Praise for *By the Shore*

"Completely delightful."—Fay Weldon

"*By the Shore* is astoundingly well-written. Craze doesn't drop topical references, nor does she patronize her narrator as adults taking on a child's voice often do. In fact, she never falters. . . . Craze has created an ageless coming-of-age story."—*Seattle Weekly*

"In May, Craze has crafted a fully realized portrait of a young girl who is leaving her childhood behind. . . . In its tender, playful final moment, the novel opens into a world after childhood, yet inspired by its promise."—*The National Post* (Canada)

"Craze draws these characters with a feathery touch, just light enough to trace the essentials without leaving a smudge."—*Los Angeles Times*

"*By the Shore* is a beautifully realized evocation of a child's world, a glimpse into an experience not yet sufficiently explored: the life of a child of a child of the 60's. This book is entirely original, full of rich detail and a slant and quirky wit."—Mary Gordon

"Craze paints a gentle picture of the vulnerability and venom of childhood. . . . *By the Shore* [is] an amusing, gritty debut which has rightly been making waves in the literary world."
—*The Independent on Sunday* (London)

"Intelligent . . . Moving . . . An impressive and thoughtful debut."
—*The Guardian* (London)

"Craze's odd, lovely book . . . patiently floats along in its own strange sea. . . . [Its] charm lies in Craze's slightly skewed perspective, the way she tells things 'slant,' as Emily Dickinson put it."
—*Time Out New York*

"Lovely and understated . . . Rarely has an author captured the thoughts and emotions of a painfully sensitive, precocious adolescent girl so well."—*The Austin Chronicle*

"*By the Shore* is one of the better books by any new writer on the scene at the moment. . . . A truly skillful novel."
—*The Express* (London)

"The pure beauty of [*By the Shore*] is in the author's ability to convey monumental moments in a girl's life with minimal action."
—*The Oakland Press*

"The great thing about Craze's vision is that although she is so clear-sighted about the traumas of adolescence . . . she also manages to remind you of that strange, fizzy joy that most of us remember from our teenage days."—*Vogue* (Britain)

BY THE SHORE

A NOVEL BY

Galaxy Craze

Grove Press / New York

Published simultaneously in Canada
Printed in the United States of America

FIRST PAPERBACK EDITION

Library of Congress Cataloging-in-Publication Data

Craze, Galaxy.
By the shore / Galaxy Craze.
p. cm.
ISBN 0-8021-3687-7 (pbk.)
I. Title.
PR6053.R378B98 1999
823'.914—dc21   98-50520
                                          CIP

DESIGN BY LAURA HAMMOND HOUGH

Grove Press
841 Broadway
New York, NY 10003

00 01 02   10 9 8 7 6 5 4 3 2 1

For my grandmother Polly Smith,
my mother Sophy Craze
and in loving memory of my grandmother
Hannah Craze

BY
THE
SHORE

One

It can be dangerous to live by the shore. In the winter, after a storm, things wash up on it: rusty pieces of sharp metal, glass, jellyfish. You must be careful where you tread. Sometimes I see a lone fish that has suffocated on the shore and think for days that there are fish in the water waiting for it to return. Then I think, There is nowhere to be safe.

But in the summer, when the guests are here, there are different things in the sand: suntan lotion, coins, and flip-flops. I even found a silver watch and it was still ticking. Once I found what I thought was a piece of skin buried in the sand. I made my brother Eden pick it up with a twig and put it in a jar of water.

This house used to be a girls' school. It had a bareness, which was its beauty. There were rusty coat hooks in the front hall and wooden cubbyholes with the names of the girls etched in them.

My mother, my brother Eden, and I moved here from London two years ago. I was ten, then, and Eden was four. When we first walked into the house, I thought, There is so much room, I can do whatever I want; I can do cartwheels down the hallways. But then we moved into the old headmistress's flat on the top floor, which had small rooms and slanted ceilings. The rest of the house was for the guests. Annabel, my mother's friend from London, came to help decorate; she hung curtains and put soap dishes in the bathrooms.

In the summer all the rooms are full. People come to swim in the sea, to sunbathe on the rocks. During the autumn and winter hardly anyone comes to stay, and I move into one of the empty guest rooms at the bottom of the house.

One afternoon, near the end of October, I came home from school and all my books, clothes and china animals had been moved. As I stood in the doorway, I thought, I must have walked into the wrong room. A broom lay on the floor next to a dustpan. The sheets had been taken off the bed. The windows were open and the rain was coming in.

I walked out of the room along the stone passageway and the steps that led to the back staircase. Then I walked up three flights of stairs, to our flat at the top of the house, to find my mother.

She was in the kitchen making tea. Annabel, who was visiting from London, sat at the table holding a cigarette.

"I thought I heard elephant footsteps," Annabel said, when she saw me. I didn't look at her.

"What have you done to my room?" My mother had her back to me. She was pouring water into the teapot. Eden sat on the floor, practising his handwriting.

"I did nothing. Annabel put everything in a box."

"Why?"

"A guest wants it. Would you like a cup of tea?" She put the pot on the table and sat down.

"Why don't you put the guest in one of the rooms on the first floor?" I asked, standing with my arms crossed. I had the feeling she had done this to spite me.

"He wanted the quietest rooms in the house. You can stay in one of the others if you want."

"I can't sleep there." It was true; some nights I would hear the sound of opera music below us. I would sit up in bed and listen. I heard what sounded like a party coming from the guest sitting room on the first floor: voices and the clink of glasses, a fire crackling and someone's laugh. But when I looked, walking slowly down the stairs, the room went quiet. It was dark and there was no one in it.

"I'm sorry, darling, but we need the money."

"He's not going to like that dungeon when he sees it," Annabel said. I liked Annabel; she brought the city with her.

"He's a writer," my mother said.

"A writer?" Annabel said. "You didn't tell me. Who is it?"

My mother was mixing butter and honey with a knife on her plate. She looked confused.

"Well, what did he sound like?" Annabel asked.

"Who?"

"The writer."

"I never spoke to him. A woman phoned and made the bookings."

"His wife?" Annabel asked.

"How long is he planning on staying?" I asked. I sat down at the table with them. I wanted some tea.

"She said until Christmas." She spread the mixed-up butter and honey on a piece of bread and cut it in half. I took one of the pieces.

"Do you think he's famous?" Annabel asked. "I do love a star in the house."

...

Annabel took Eden and me to see *Fantasia.* When the film ended she said she fancied a sausage roll. We drove to the shop, but it was closed. I remembered it was Sunday night, and I had two lots of maths homework to do. We drove home in the drizzle.

When we arrived back at the house there was a woman standing outside the door. The rain was thicker now and she had wedged herself in the corner of the doorway, trying not to get wet.

At first I thought she was the crazy woman from London, asking to use the loo. During the summer holidays I spent a week with Annabel in London. In the middle of the afternoon a woman rang the bell. When Annabel said hello, the woman asked if she could use the loo. "Is she mad?" Annabel asked me, and we peeked out of the window to see what she looked like. All we saw was the back of her, bright yellow hair and a skirt suit that made her look like a stewardess. Then she came back the next day and asked again.

"Hello!" the woman by the door shouted to us as we were getting out of the car. "Are you Lucy?"

"No, I'm not," Annabel said.

"Do you know where she is? I've been ringing the bell for at least ten minutes but no one's answering." She was wearing a shiny black raincoat and high leather boots.

"The bell is broken." Annabel grabbed Eden by the wrist and walked quickly towards the door, as though they were crossing a busy street. "Are you here for a room?" she asked, as she opened the door and let her inside.

"Yes," the woman said as she tried to brush the raindrops from her coat. "I phoned the other day about two rooms." Then I knew who she was, the one who wanted the quietest ones.

"Oh, for the writer?" Annabel turned to me with a bounce and said, "Be an angel and find your mother, will you?" I stood there. They were both looking at me. I was trying to leave but I couldn't move. I felt so heavy.

"Well, hurry up," Annabel said, and gave me a push on the back that got me going.

The staircase was long and made of dark wood. I walked slowly. The air was thick from the rain.

My mother was sitting on the sofa in our sitting room, a cup of tea in her hand. She had her back to me.

"There's a woman downstairs."

I could see the top of her head jerk up.

"Christ," she said. Then she stood up and looked at me. "Don't come up behind me like that." She had spilled her tea; it was running down her arm and onto her shirt. She held the hand with the cup out as though it were being pulled by a string.

"Get me something," she said.

"There's a woman downstairs waiting for you," I said again.

"I have to change," she said, unbuttoning her shirt. "It's one of my favourite shirts, you know. Run down and tell her I'll be right there."

I didn't go back downstairs. I went into the kitchen to get something to eat. There were three baked potatoes on the stove that were still warm. I took one and cut it in half and put salt and pieces of butter in it, and then I closed it back up and waited for the butter to melt. I stood there with my hands wrapped around the potato. My stomach hurt. I thought about the polar bear in the zoo, the way he walks back and forth against the bars of his cage, back and forth, up and down. Every day he must wonder, How did this happen, and when will it end?

Two

My mother woke me at six for school the next morning. She sat on the edge of my bed and rubbed her hands in a circle on my back. "Do you want an egg and soldiers for breakfast?" she asked. I pretended to sleep so she would keep rubbing. "I'll bring you a cup of tea."

When she left, I got out of bed. It was still dark outside. I opened my wardrobe to get my uniform, but it wasn't there. I went into the kitchen to see if it was hanging over the stove; it wasn't. I went to the bathroom and found it in the laundry basket surrounded by socks and dirty knickers. I picked it out. It looked awful: crumpled and smelly, the white shirt nearly grey, two buttons missing. I threw it on the floor.

"I can't go to school today." I yelled this at my mother. I was already angry because I really thought she would try to make me wear it. She would think it was funny, breaking the rules.

"Why not?"

"My uniform is too dirty. Look at it! It's all dirty and wrinkled. I can't wear it." This was true; we were not allowed to go to school in dirty clothes.

"Wash it now and you can go after lunch, then." She sat at the round wooden table, eating her egg. She was wearing a short nightgown with a sweatshirt pulled over it and her old dirty flat moccasins. Eden was already dressed and sitting quietly and straight in the chair next to hers, carefully dipping a strip of toast into his egg.

"Eat your breakfast before it gets cold." A place was set for me: a brown egg, sitting in a pink eggcup, a piece of brown toast cut in strips in a saucer. I sat down to eat. We were all very quiet; it was a grey morning and the rest of the house was still asleep.

Eden raised an arm and threw the piece of toast that he had been examining to the floor.

"What did you just do?" my mother asked.

He was staring at the floor, blowing his cheeks out, his face turning red. He didn't answer.

"He's choking. Oh, my God, he's choking!" She pulled him off his chair and banged him on the back. She always thought he was about to die.

"Get off of me!" he yelled, flinging his thin arms at her. "There was white on it!"

"What?"

"The white got on it! You didn't cook it enough!" he said. His face was still red.

"Well, why didn't you just pick it off?" she asked, trying to calm him down.

"Because he's scared of it," I said, leaning forward to look at him. "Aren't you? Last night he wouldn't walk down the stairs because he saw a ball of dust floating around and he started shaking. Didn't you?"

"Stop it. I've already got a headache, so just don't you start too," my mother said, loudly. We went silent. She took her cup of tea and stood up. "You are a ridiculous child, Eden. What do you think the white is going to do to you?"

"I don't like it." He looked at the ground.

"He's choking, he's choking!" I said, in her panicked voice. This made him laugh.

"Right. I'm going to put my coat on. Then we'll be off, so get ready. I've got a headache now." When she spoke like this she was trying to sound like a different mother. She left the room to get her coat.

My brother stood next to his chair. I sat across the table from him. His uniform had been washed and ironed. His straight brown hair was combed over to the side; he had his school hat in his hand. He looked perfect.

We were alone. I ate my toast and swung my legs under the chair, humming.

"Aren't you going to school today?" he asked me.

I stuck my finger in my egg, walked around the table, and wiped it on the back of his navy blue jacket. He saw me coming; he stood still, his eyes wide, he let me do it. He dropped his hat and opened his mouth. I ran out of the room.

...

I went to the bathroom and filled the sink with warm water and soap. Too much soap, but I wanted it clean. I was feeling mean; my breath was short. First I washed the white shirt, then the blue dress in the leftover water. That was something my grandmother had taught me: never waste water or toilet paper. She had caught me once, leaving the tap running while I brushed my teeth. She slapped my fingers and turned it off tightly, saying,"That's what those American girls all do." She knew about them, the Americans; she had married one, a businessman with three daughters.

I scrubbed the collar together and the sleeve cuffs that had pencil marks on them. Everyone complained about the uniform, but I liked it.

...

At the school I went to in London, before we moved here, we were allowed to wear whatever we liked. My mother dressed me in striped overalls and boots. I had short hair. It had been long, past my shoulders, until her friend Gary, the hairdresser, came over. "Let him cut your hair," my mother told me. "He's the most fashionable hairdresser in London. He cut Mick Jagger's hair last week."

It was the end of the summer; the air coming in through the windows was still damp and warm. I was used to staying up late with her friends, doing what they wanted, fetching ashtrays, putting the kettle on, and now getting my hair cut. I sat on a stool. It took a long time; they were smoking and talking. I must have fallen asleep because I didn't see it until the next morning when I went into my mother's room. She was in bed asleep and he was next to her. They were under the covers, naked. I could tell. The room smelled. The mirror was on the floor, leaning against a chair. I sat down to look at my hair. It was short, messy, like a boy's. I was so angry. I had lost something. I started crying, right there on the floor, with the hairdresser in the bed.

"It looks really great," Gary said, leaning up on his elbows, his bare chest showing.

"It's ugly," I said. That word "ugly" felt so right. Square and heavy.

"Stop feeling so sorry for yourself, it'll grow," my mother said, laying her face on his chest. I thought she liked to embarrass me in front of men. It made her seem more like an older sister than a mother. She was twenty seven then and I was eight.

I kept thinking about how she said "feeling sorry for yourself". Those words were like a slap, and every time I heard them in my head I felt myself blush. I sat on the floor of my room with my legs crossed and just sat. My mother came in and asked if I wanted to go out for breakfast with them. I shook my head. She told me my hair looked "really great". I didn't say anything, and she came over and kissed me on the top of my head. When I knew they were gone I jumped up and ran to the mirror again. I liked to watch myself cry.

Later, when I began to feel calm and watery, I went to the kitchen and ate some Weetabix with milk. I streamed honey over it and waited for it to get soggy. I ate it and then I really panicked.

I was starting my new school in a week and I remembered how I wanted to look: straight hair in one plait down my back, flopping when I walked. A little careless, a little brazen: a girl from a safe home. I had thought about it all summer, every day. A plait down my back, tidy, with a hair elastic, not just a beige rubber band. Sometimes a ribbon. I would wake up early and do it myself, I was good with hair, but I would tell everyone my mum did it. "She makes me," I would tell them.

The first day at my new school I was standing at my cubbyhole, organizing my markers. A girl walked over and asked, "Are you a boy or a girl?"

I was too embarrassed to tell my mother what the girl had said. The next day I wore a dress and sandals. "Why aren't you wearing your boots?" my mother asked. "They're ugly," I said, my new word.

"They're cool," she said. "All my friends love them."

...

I wrung the water from my uniform and hung it in the kitchen where it was warm. My mother had taken Eden to school. Everything was still on the table, freezing into place. I wondered what I could do until my uniform dried. I still had my maths homework, but I didn't want to do it; I would probably never do it. I picked up the plates, eggcups, teacups, and spoons from the table, put them in the sink, and washed them.

...

Her name was Patricia. "Patricia," she said. "Not Patty." She came to make sure everything was arranged and to look at the rooms. To make sure there were enough sockets for an extra lamp and the typewriter.

"There's no phone in the room," Patricia told my mother.

"No, everyone uses this one. There won't be a queue now."

My mother pointed to the pay phone above the desk. We were standing in the front hall by the desk where the postman leaves the post. Patricia looked at the phone. Her eyes stayed on it for a moment, and she nodded slowly.

"Is he writing a book?" my mother asked.

"Yes. I'm helping with the research. I must find out what time the train leaves. I have to get back to the office." She said the word "office" like it was a really important place.

"Are you his wife?" my mother asked. I was wondering if my mother thought she was pretty.

"Not yet," she said quickly. She stuck her thumbnail in her mouth and stood for a moment looking at the ceiling.

"Oh, there is one thing I wanted to ask you."

"What's that?" My mother seemed worried. She thought Patricia was going to ask her to lower the price of the rooms.

"Come here and I'll show you." She led us towards the back staircase. I thought she was going to take us to the rooms downstairs, but she turned into a narrow passage that led to the coatroom and to a tiny toilet that only flushed once a day. I thought, Why would she have come back here? She walked fast; she knew where she was going.

"These!" she said loudly, and pointed. She looked like a child. "These! I just absolutely love them." She was pointing at four charcoal drawings of horses hanging on the wall. We've had them forever; they were in my mother's bedroom in London. "I have always loved horses," she said, turning to my mother.

"Do you have a horse?" I asked. I wanted her to pay attention to me.

"Not a real one, but I had a collection of toy horses. My whole room was covered in posters of them." She took a deep breath, as though she were trying to smell them, and stood quietly for a moment.

Toy horses. Posters of horses. That type of girl, that type of woman.

"And that's why I thought it would be nice if I could move them into our room." She was staring at them.

"You mean move them into your bedroom?" my mother asked.

I had never really noticed the drawings here in this thin, dim hall, but suddenly I wanted them in my room too.

"They look good here," I said loudly to my mother.

"Since he's staying for such a long time and those rooms are so bland. These would cheer it up a bit."

I looked at the drawings again. They were not cheery. In one, the horse looked like a growling dog.

"We have some other pictures in the attic. The ones Granny sent of the pears and flowers." My mother said the last part to me. She was getting nervous. A boy my mother had been friends with in school drew the horses. The thought of them in a stranger's room bothered her.

"No, no. I know just what you're talking about. My mother has prints like that too. He wouldn't like them, but he would like these, I know. And he should have something to look at. It must get boring just sitting over a desk all day, banging at the typewriter." She held her hands out in front of her and wiggled her fingers as though she were typing.

My mother stood staring at the pictures. Then she said, "How would we get a nail into those stone walls?"

"I think they look good here," I said again. I thought of the boy. He was ten when he drew them. My mother thought he was dead now.

"I can figure it out," Patricia said. "Just lend me a hammer." But I could tell, by the way my mother crossed her arms, looking over at her with half closed eyes, that she would not let her have them.

...

I was still wondering if my mother thought she was pretty. I did. In London, sometimes, we had an all-girls night. My mother's two best girlfriends, Annabel and Suzy, would come over; they'd open a bottle of wine and talk and cook. I would sit on the kitchen floor near the stove, where it was warm, and listen.

"And what do you think of that new one he's got?" my mother asked Suzy one time.

"She's such a bore. She came round the pub last Wednesday. All she did was smoke my fags and put her lipstick on and wipe it off and then put it on again. Three times she did it. I was counting. Three times, at the table, I promise you; I'm not joking." She was rolling a joint.

"Was he with her?" my mother asked.

"He didn't sit next to her."

"Well, is she pretty?" My mother was really listening. She had her spoon in the sauce but hadn't stirred it once.

"I think she's boring, but the men probably like her, all they see is that bright hair and her little bottom. They have the simplest tastes. Be an angel and get me a glass of water, will you?" she asked me.

"You know what she looks like?" Annabel had it figured out; we were all listening now. She poured herself some wine and said, "A shampoo model, she looks like a bloody shampoo model." They thought this was the funniest thing they had ever heard. They said it all night about everyone, even the men. "Now he," they said, bursting, "he looks like a shampoo model!" Then they'd start laughing again.

I looked through a magazine to find the shampoo ads. Girls with waist-length hair, brown or blonde, a middle parting, walking though a field of daisies. Clean, neat, quiet noses, smelling like the magazine perfume. They were pretty. I didn't see what was so funny. Patricia looked like one of them.

Three

Patricia phoned a taxi to collect her and take her to the station, back to London. It was noon and my uniform that I had hung up over the stove was dry. I ironed it on top of a towel on my bedroom floor. Then I dressed. When I came out, my mother was in the bathroom running a bath.

"Aren't you going to drive me?" I asked through the door.

"My bath will get cold."

The drive winds between the bushes and the trees. It's almost a mile long; we measured it once. With the sound of the wind and the waves, it's hard to hear a car coming ahead or behind you. My mother thinks that sometimes I go deaf, so I keep safely to the side, half in the twigs and thorns, as close as a cat.

...

One night in our flat in London, my mother and I were making mashed potatoes when Annabel and Suzy dropped by.

"I brought us a little something," Suzy said, as she walked into the kitchen. She pulled a small packet wrapped in tinfoil out of her bag and held it up in the air, wiggling it between two fingers. When I stood up to look, she closed it up in her hand. "Not for children," she said, pointing her nose at me. I was the only child then; it was before Eden had been born.

"You didn't. Who did you get it from?" Annabel asked.

"Gary, your hairdresser. It was a real bargain."

My mother walked out of the kitchen with the bowl of potatoes for me to peel.

"Let's get you set up out here, then." She unfolded old newspapers on the floor and put the bowl down on them. This is the way we had dyed Easter eggs. "Just peel them onto the paper and put them in the bowl. And take out the eyes."

I sat cross-legged on the floor and counted the potatoes. There were seven. The kitchen door was open a crack and I could hear them whispering, I sat quietly, listening to see if it was me they were whispering about. I held a potato in my hand, each peel a small tug. The streetlamp shone in through the window like a gold shell. They forgot to whisper, and soon I could hear every word they said in the kitchen; they were talking loud and fast and not about me. It became a race. They could hardly wait for one to finish a sentence before the next would jump on the end of the last word and take off like a relay runner.

They were talking about men. My mother was going on about her date with Paul. He picked her up in the convertible he had borrowed from his manager. She wore her old jeans, that she had to lie down to do up, and all night the zipper stuck into her stomach like a little nail. He hadn't tried to spend the night, so she wasn't sure if he liked her.

Annabel poked her head out the door. "All right?"

I had only peeled one potato, I had mud on my hands. "What happens if you eat a potato eye?" I asked, pretending to be concentrating. I didn't want them to think I was interested in them.

"I can't remember," she said, and went back in the kitchen. There was more talking. Then the phone rang. It was him, Paul.

There was a party tonight. "Well, we're sort of in for the evening," I heard my mother say. "Maybe I'll pop by later. Give me the address, just in case." She hung up the phone and turned the stove off; I heard the click.

"We have to hurry, he might leave soon," my mother said, her voice high and sparkling.

"What about the food?" Annabel asked.

"Just leave it. Come on, let's go; it's in Shepherd's Bush."

My mother walked out of the kitchen, straight and fast. "Come on, you two, hurry up."

Annabel and Suzy followed behind in a pair.

"Look at me, I look like Mrs Mop." Suzy was staring at herself in the hall mirror.

"We'll just look like we don't really care; you know, like we just stopped by on our walk." She could do this, my mother, make everything seem casual.

"Our walk where?" Annabel said, putting on her coat. It was white plastic and belted at the waist. "You haven't even got a dog."

"Okay, how do I look?" my mother asked me.

She was wearing a tiny tight brown leather jacket with a huge boa of yellow fur and feathers around the collar and wrists.

"Like an Eskimo."

"Oh, very nice. An Eskimo! Thanks a lot, darling." She searched in her coat pockets. "Have I got everything? Don't turn the oven on, May, and if anyone phones me write it down on a piece of paper."

Suzy's coat looked like a patchwork quilt. She was standing in front of the hall mirror back-combing her hair.

"Don't eat all the sweets and make yourself sick again, and don't play with matches," Annabel said, as she put on shimmery pink lipstick. I already knew this. It is something I had always known: to be careful.

My mother came over to where I was sitting with the potatoes and kissed me on the top of my head. "Mr Brompton's next door if you need anything."

"You didn't leave an iron on, did you?" Annabel asked.

They gathered in front of the door like three little dogs waiting to be let out.

"Okay. Keys, money, fags?" my mother said, and the three of them felt in their pockets.

Everything was fine and they were ready to leave. My mother locked the door behind her, I heard the click.

I was alone in the house with the half-cooked food. I walked around looking for a clock; I wanted to know what time it was. I looked out of the window and saw the three of them go down the street. My mother was in front, walking fast, hurrying them along, rushing to see a boy. It was a cold night, a quiet street. A teenage boy and girl sat across the street on some steps sharing a cigarette. I saw my mother look back once as she walked ahead. When they turned the corner, I closed the window. Inside, my face stung from the cold in the heat.

I wanted to boil the potatoes and eat them with butter and salt. I was hungry but afraid of the stove. I didn't understand fire, that it had to cling to burn; I thought it could just leap through the air.

I went to find a clock in my mother's room. It was half past nine. Above her bed on the yellow wall were the horse pictures, watching me while I looked through her drawers for chocolate.

My bedroom in London was behind a Victorian paste screen, in a corner of the sitting room. I had a box under my bed. In it were two dolls, dolls' clothes, five grey toy mice, and some doll's house furniture: a red sofa with yellow spots, a wooden table, and a packet of knives and forks. Tiny ones. Too small for the dolls, but the right size for the mice.

I sat down with my box in front of me and made the mice and the dolls a house. One of the dolls was an ice-skater; the other one, with long brown hair, was a horse rider. The mice lived beneath them, the way mice do.

At some point I must have left my room and walked around the flat, gathering things.

I was back on the floor when my mother walked in.

"You're awake." She stood in her coat, holding the front door keys in her hand. "Why didn't you answer the phone? I let it ring thirty times, at least thirty times. Why didn't you pick it up?"

I had been sitting on my heels with my back bent, looking at the floor. When I tried to move my feet, they were numb.

"What?" I looked up at her.

"Why didn't you answer the phone?" She was staring down at me.

"I never heard the phone."

"You never heard the phone. I only rang three times. I know what you were doing. I know. You just sat here and listened and wanted me to worry, didn't you?"

I was sure I hadn't heard the phone ring. I was sure. It was something I would have done—sit and let it ring—but I had never thought of it.

"It didn't ring," I said.

She turned and left, walking heavily into the sitting room, where she picked up the phone, listened, put it down; picked it up, dialled the operator, asked her to phone back. It rang.

"See, it works," she said, back in my room standing over me, hands on her hips. Her lipstick had worn off except at the corners of her mouth, and there were smears of black mascara under her eyes, where her lashes touched the skin.

"What time is it?"

"I don't know, May. You had me really worried." She took her eyes off me and stood silent for a moment as she looked around the room.

"What?" I asked, getting up. She stood completely still.

"What is this? All these little pieces of rubbish on the floor. Why do you play with little bits and pieces? This looks like a German flea market."

The floor was covered except for the spot where I had been sitting. Tea bags, chopsticks, cotton balls, folded-up pieces of loo paper, a large shell filled with water. I could not tell what it was now, but it had been something—a whole town, a whole house, a bathroom; the shell was the tub. It had order. It had been lived in. It had really been something. But now, standing up next to her, looking down like birds, it was only a mess.

"You must be deaf." She was looking at me again. "Are you deaf?"

"No." What if I was? That would be something. An illness, a doctor, a special school. "She was very clever, considering . . ." my teachers would say.

"Well, obviously you are. First thing in the morning we're going to the doctor."

A man entered from the other side of the screen. He had straight thick brown hair that hung around his face like a shawl.

"There you are," my mother said. "This is my friend Paul." She was speaking softer now. Her friend Paul. "This is May."

He looked at me, nodded, then raised his hand slowly, as though he were pulling it up from a puddle of glue. It quickly fell back down, and he stood with his long arms hanging forward for a moment. Suddenly his head jerked up and he looked around, surprised. "I think I should get some water."

"That man is drunk," I told my mother, in a low voice that reminded me of my grandmother.

"No, he's not drunk." She said the word "drunk" as though it were falling from a high board. "No one gets drunk any more. Anyway, he happens to be a rock star."

...

The school here sat behind the chapel, near a hedge, like an old tomb. The sky was thick and grey above me. Engraved above the two tall heavy wooden doorways, like the names of heroes, were BOYS and GIRLS. But now, since the village had grown, it was an all-girls' school.

I walked along the stone path, past the chapel, towards the school. There was no one around, and I sat down on a wooden bench by the front gates. It was lunchtime; everyone was in the dining hall, and the smell of pudding was in the chapel garden. I thought about my mother's friend, the boy who drew those horse pictures.

When my mother was nine she moved to a new town. The other girls in her form had all been together since they were six and would not let go of each other's hands to let her in their circle, so she became friends with a boy who was a year older. They met at the shop on her way home from school, where she bought honey and cream ice lollies and he bought a bag of crisps, because cold things hurt his teeth.

The girls were let out half an hour earlier than the boys, so every day she would sit on the steps and wait for him. One afternoon she waited until one of the last boys in his class said, as he walked down the steps, "He got sick."

He'd been in a running race with some other boys. It had rained that day, and the floors were wet from the Wellingtons and coats: wet green stone school floors. They had begun near the window and raced the whole way down the corridor to the radiator. They took off, each with a silver ball of determination, and ran to the end. When he tried to stop he slipped forward, crashing into the edge of the hot radiator with his head.

He couldn't speak; he couldn't remember anything. He was put in the special children's hospital. Later that year my mother's parents moved to London, and she never saw him again.

Four

One night the phone rang. It was late; everyone was asleep. The phone rang and rang because my mother couldn't find it in the dark.

Paul, my mother's rock-star boyfriend in London, used to do this: Phone at three in the morning, ring the doorbell at six in the morning. He didn't care about waking us up. He would leave the flat in the middle of the night when we were asleep and leave the door unlocked behind him. I would hear him putting on his shoes, walking to the door, bumping into things. When I was sure he was gone I would get out of bed and lock the door. There was no safety with him around. I went to make sure it wasn't him phoning us here.

I stood next to my mother in the kitchen. She had the phone in her hand. The light was on, making us squint.

"We're terribly, terribly sorry. The taxi company is closed." I heard a man's voice coming through the receiver. It was the writer and Patricia; they were stranded at the station.

When she put the phone down, she looked at me and said, "Who takes trains this late? Come to the station with me."

I shook my head.

"Please! I don't want to drive all alone in the dark."

"Wake up Annabel," I said.

"She'll take too long to get ready. Anyway, she needs to stay here in case Eden wakes up."

I crossed my arms in front of me.

"Please come with me. Come on. It'll be fun, we'll listen to the radio. We'll stop off and get a bun and tea."

I have heard her like this before: desperate, needing company. "I'll pay the taxi if you come over. We have ice cream," she would say, trying to bribe her friends.

I was looking at my toes. I had my blue nightgown on with white lace around the collar. When I first saw it I thought I could also wear it as a dress. But everyone could tell; everyone knew it was only a nightgown.

"The stupid bun shop won't even be open yet," I said.

This stopped her for a moment; then she said, "Just put a jumper on over your nightgown. Come on, darling, hurry up!" She was speaking loudly, trying to make me think this would be exciting.

I was too old to walk around in my thinning nightgown in front of a strange man. People watch my body now with a steady curiosity, the way I watched tadpoles in a jar. It makes me shy and I slouch, and then my back aches. There are girls, in my form, who like to show it off.

"My feet are cold," I said, and went into my room to get dressed. I wore a vest under my shirt and put on my corduroys and a striped cardigan.

We walked across the gravel to the car. It had rained, and now the air was damp. I could see the moon on the wet shiny ground, and the last orange and yellow leaves.

I waited outside the car while she turned the engine on. I wanted to see the lights go up and reflect on the ground but I didn't tell her this, it was too small a thing. I knelt down and pretended I was taking a stone out of my shoe.

As we drove to the station, the raindrops on the windows stretched and blew away. The overgrown hedges on the side of the road scraped against the windows like fingers in a scary movie. For a long time we were alone, the only car on the narrow winding lanes.

This is what it was like here: handing out keys, walking guests to the bedroom, changing the sheets, putting keys back on their hooks, and now this—driving in the middle of the night to pick them up from the railway station.

Everything—the sea, the house, the rocks, the clean towels—was for them. Not good enough to live in, too far from the city, too damp in the winter, but nice enough for the weekend, the week, the month.

They were standing in front of the beamed station house, a pair in raincoats in the night, standing together.

My mother stopped the car and moved her head forward, looking at them through the glass. She would have stared all night. She stares at couples on the street; she turns her head and looks, the way people who have lost a dog must look at every dog that passes by. Checking, making sure it's not theirs.

"That's them, obviously," I said, annoyed. They were the only ones there and so were we. She opened the door and stepped out.

"Come on, then," she whispered to me.

I shook my head and stayed in the car. She was wearing her moccasins, the grey T-shirt dress she slept in, and an old tweed coat over it. All the buttons had fallen off the coat, so she held it closed with one hand and waved hello with the other.

I saw him lean forward to shake my mother's hand. He was tall and had dark brown hair. Then they picked up their bags and walked towards the car. I could hear him apologize. "I am so sorry," he was saying. "Our train got stuck for five hours. Do you want me to drive? You must be tired."

"No. Thank you," my mother said. I heard the car boot slam shut. I leaned against the door with my hair flung over my eyes, pretending to be asleep. I could still do things like that: pretend to fall asleep and not wake up. It was easy, especially in front of people who didn't have children, and they didn't. I knew that, I could tell; they wouldn't have taken such a late train.

They sat in the back seat. Someone put a seat belt on; I heard it click into the buckle. I heard Patricia yawn, and he apologized again.

My mother said, "This is my daughter, May."

"I know May. Is she really asleep?" Patricia asked, leaning forward to look at me.

The car was muggy. Hot air was blowing from the vent and the windows fogged.

"Should I move my seat up?" my mother asked. His knees must have been poking into the back of her seat.

"No, I'm fine. Thank you." He had a nice voice. It wasn't demanding to be heard, it was sitting in a corner, not thrown out from the head of the table.

It was quiet in the car; on the drive home no one spoke. The only sound was the engine and the wind coming through the cracks in the windows and Patricia's little yawns. It made me nervous when no one spoke. I was wide awake with my eyes closed. I opened one eye a tiny bit and peeked out. My mother was sitting upright, staring straight ahead of her with both hands on the wheel. This made me feel safe. She usually sat in the driver's seat as if she were lounging in a hammock, with a mug of tea in her hand, looking around, turning the knob on the radio. I saw her open her mouth as though she was going to say something, but she didn't.

Finally I could smell the sea. I only notice it when I'm gone and then come back. We were close to home.

"I can smell the sea," he said, from the back.

"Sand is the best pumice stone," Patricia said. "Walking on the beach barefoot. It's just the absolute best." The car was finally still, the engine turned off. I felt the cold air coming through the open doors. I was tired now. Someone opened my door and bent over me.

"Should I carry her?" It was him. I felt his breath on my face; it was warm. I wanted to be carried, I tried to look small. He bent down and put his hands underneath me, the way you lift a small baby or a seven-year-old whose head is flung back and who's really asleep. He lifted me carefully out of the car, I felt his fingers against my back ribs.

"No, don't worry, you don't have to carry her," I heard my mother say. Her voice sounded soft against the sea.

"You'll hurt your back! Put that girl down. She's too big to carry!" Patricia said, whispering in his ear.

"Where's her room?" he asked my mother, as he moved away from Patricia.

He walked towards the house. My mother opened the door and led him up the three flights of stairs into our flat. He put me down on the bottom bunk, gently slipping his hands out from underneath me. I heard him hit his head on the top bunk when he stood up.

"Are you all right?" my mother asked.

"Ouch." He thought it was funny. I could hear him trying not to laugh. Someone took off my shoes, I think it was my mother. I was trying to keep my eyelids very still. If you are really asleep, your eyelids don't flutter.

Five

The next day Jolene came home with me after school. It was Friday, and she was going to spend the night. As we walked towards the house I saw Annabel standing by the hedge, talking to the writer.

"I come up here to find antiques for my decorating business," I could hear Annabel say, as she wrapped and unwrapped a paisley-patterned shawl around her shoulders. "And then I take them back to London and add a zero." Her voice was like a hat full of feathers when she spoke to him.

"It's beautiful here," he said. "Such a strange old house." There was something about the way he looked, like a hollow tree, standing there staring at the house.

Jolene and I stepped forward. The gravel crunched underneath us; our satchels hung over our shoulders. I saw him look towards us and I looked down, away from him. I couldn't look up. He had held me in his arms; he had carried me into bed like a baby, and I had let him. I had wanted him to.

I led Jolene the long way round so I wouldn't have to walk near him. "That's the man who's staying in my room downstairs." We walked very close to each other, side by side, our shoulders touching. She looked back at him, over her shoulder. We went to the side of the house where the tallest trees grew, three of them in a circle. We put our satchels down on the grass and stood in the middle and waited for the wind to blow. We had to catch twelve falling leaves by the end of autumn. It would bring us good luck. What I wished for when I looked up at the golden and orange leaves was that something in me would change, that I would be different in school, louder and fun, and not have a twisting feeling in my stomach whenever I walked past girls like Barbara Whitmore and her friends. I held my hands out waiting, looking up. So did Jolene, her hands and her eyes towards the tree. She started laughing, her round face and her perfectly straight hair, cut just below her ears, shaking from her laughter.

"What?"

"Remember when we were singing and that man put cotton in his ears—" She broke off suddenly. Patricia came jogging towards us.

"Hi, May," Patricia said. She stopped running. She wore a pink unitard and bright white shoes, with her straight blond hair in a high ponytail and a towelling band around her forehead.

"This is Jolene, my friend from school."

"Best friend," Jolene said.

"Where's your mother? I went upstairs to look for her but she wasn't there," Patricia said.

"I haven't seen her."

"Oh." She looked over at the ground where our satchels lay at the bottom of the trees. "Is that kitchen downstairs for the guests?"

I nodded.

"All right, then." And she jogged off around the house. I thought she must just be running round and round the house.

"She's pretty," Jolene said. She had stopped laughing and stood very still, looking after Patricia as she ran away from us.

"She's that man's girlfriend," I said.

"She probably has lots of lipsticks and perfume bottles and things like that." Jolene's voice sounded as though it were getting further and further away, and she kept staring.

When we were inside the house, instead of going upstairs we walked towards the passage that led downstairs. We just wanted to look inside her room, Patricia's room, to see it. The air felt cold against the stone walls. I thought, Now my mother will have to turn up the expensive heat.

There were only two rooms downstairs and they were across the hall from each other. The door to one of the rooms was half open, and when we looked inside there was someone in it. It was my mother. She had her back to us. I waited for her to move, to turn around, to do something. I thought, What is she doing? She was just standing there in the middle of the room.

"Mum!" It echoed against the stone walls. She jumped the way you do when you touch an electric fence.

"Don't do that!" she said, turning around, catching her breath. She was wearing jeans and a navy jumper. Her hair was off her face in a ponytail, neatly, no bumps and no pieces hanging down.

"Sorry," I said, but only because Jolene was there. "What are you doing?"

"Checking. Making sure they have enough towels and everything." She held her hands together in front of her. They were shaking.

The bed was made, the quilt pulled over the pillows, the sheets folded over and tucked in at the corners as neat and tight as a kidskin glove. There was a suitcase on the floor, unzipped, the clothes shoved in, not folded. On the desk was a pile of large books, dictionaries and maps, a typewriter, and pens.

On the bed were two brand-new white towels with embroidered pale blue stars around the edges. They were from Bloomingdale's in New York City, America. My grandmother had sent them to me.

"What are you doing down here?" she asked us, smoothing the bedspread with her hands.

"Those are the Bloomingdale's towels." I couldn't take my eyes off them. They were mine and I had plans for them, hanging neatly in a bathroom of my own, one day when I was older, with matching blue and white soaps.

She took her hands off the bed. "What is that smell in here? It smells like . . . it reminds me of something."

Jolene and I stepped to where she was standing in the middle of the room. We took deep breaths through our noses.

"What is it?" my mother asked again.

"It smells like the soap in art class," Jolene said.

My mother carefully picked up a dark green shirt from the suitcase and held it up to her nose.

Jolene and I looked at each other, standing by the end of the bed with our arms at our side.

"Where are her things?"

"In there." My mother pointed to the closed door across the hall.

"Why aren't they staying in the same room?"

"I don't know," she said. She was chewing on the skin next to her nail.

We went upstairs. My mother moving slowly behind us.

"What are you doing?" I asked. My mother stood still, one hand wrapped around the banister.

"I'm just trying to remember something," she said softly, as though she were talking to herself.

"Oh, there you are." Patricia stood at the bottom of the stairs. Her voice sounded so full to me, so sure. "I've been looking for you."

I couldn't tell who was younger. My mother's face was more like a girl's, but the way Patricia moved and the way her voice went up, excitedly, made her seem younger.

"I just wanted to make sure I told you, before I left, not to bring Rufus breakfast in the morning."

"Oh . . . didn't he like it? The milk wasn't rotten or anything?" my mother asked.

"He doesn't want to be disturbed while he's working for any reason. He'll use the guest kitchen downstairs."

My mother shook her head, as if to say, Of course, of course. Anytime someone tells you they don't want what you have given them, no matter how small, it feels like a long pinch.

Jolene and I went upstairs to the kitchen. It was Jolene's teatime. Every day her mother made her something: cheese on toast, beans on toast, something hot. There was a loaf of brown bread on the counter. I cut two pieces of bread, buttered them, and put them on a tray with a jar of Marmite and a bottle of fizzy lemonade.

I put the food on a tray and carried it into my bedroom. Jolene sat on the bed, eating bread and Marmite and sipping her drink. I wasn't hungry. I walked around my room looking at my things. I had eight miniature china animals lined up on a thin wooden shelf nailed to the wall. It was my only collection. The other girls had collections in tins, stickers and things. Some had rosettes pinned to their walls: prize-blue, purple, white, and red ribbons. I thought they meant concentration and interest.

"Do you have any biscuits?" Jolene asked, looking up from the book.

I picked up the empty tray and carried it out of the room. I could hear laughter coming from the kitchen.

"Oh, shush!" Annabel said as I walked in, putting her finger up to her lips. "Tiptoe, tiptoe! God forbid you disturb him."

My mother was chopping up a plate of potatoes and vegetables for Eden's supper, her face red from laughing.

"Shush. We'd better whisper," my mother said, whispering. Eden sat in a chair next to Annabel. He was laughing too.

"We'd better whisper," Eden said, imitating them.

My mother put the plate down in front of Eden.

"Oh, don't chew so loudly, Eden. We don't want to disturb Shakespeare downstairs," Annabel said, and then they both started again, their shoulders shaking, cheeks turning red.

When they had calmed down, my mother took a deep breath. "Did he tell you what he's writing?" she asked.

"He's translating some old poems," Annabel said, rolling her eyes.

"Poems?"

"I was all excited. I thought Anthony Burgess was going to show up!" Annabel said.

"I think he's quite handsome."

"Quite."

"Patricia's only staying for the weekend," my mother said, but Annabel just looked at her.

I went back into my room with the biscuits and the radio. I had a picture of my father that he had given to me. He was sitting on the back of a motorcycle in white trousers, smoking a cigarette.

"My dad's much more handsome than that man," I said to Jolene. She looked up at the photo and nodded. Jolene had never met my father; he had never been here. I told people that my mother and father were still married, but my father lived in London because of his business. I knew this wasn't true, but I didn't care. I would lie to anyone to save myself, to make us seem better.

Outside it was turning a dark sweater-grey. Jolene and I sat on the floor with the radio between us, eating biscuits. We were waiting for our favourite song to come on the radio so we could learn all the words. Jolene had a piece of paper and pencil to write them down with. Song after song after song, then the advertisements, then another song, then our song. We bent forward, listening closely, trying to learn the words so we could sing it. When I stood up, my feet hurt. It was a dark night. I couldn't even see the trees against the sky. Winter was coming.

"I'm going downstairs to get my towels, Jolene," I said.

She was reading an old children's book, carefully turning the yellowing pages: *The Lonely Moon* by Elias Loon.

"Do you want to come with me?" She shook her head, looking down at the book.

I was wearing a sweatshirt and my flannel pyjama bottoms. I didn't have shoes on. Each step down my feet got colder. At the bottom of the staircase I looked down the hallway towards their rooms. Both doors were closed; light was coming through under the bottoms. The stone floors were freezing, I tiptoed down the hallway. It reminded me of being small, standing on my toes and the smell of school around me. A moment can take you somewhere, lift you up, and everything softens. Then something happens, a sound, a person, and suddenly you are yourself again, walking to a stranger's room to ask for your towels.

I stood outside his door and looked down at my stomach, smoothing my shirt with my hand. Then I knocked.

He opened the door. He stood there in yellow pyjamas, his hair dripping wet and one of my towels in his hand. It was wet, used.

"Oh," I said.

"Hi," he said.

"That's my towel and you're getting it all wet." He stepped back and stared at it, holding it out in front of him, the way my brother held the bird with the broken wing he found.

"I didn't know, I'm sorry." He looked almost scared.

Then I had nothing to say. I've been this way about things before. Once when my mother was on the phone doodling circles and hearts and stars and squares and things. "That's my pen," I told her, "and you're wasting the ink."

So I just stood in front of him. I put my hands on my hips trying to look tough, like I was just a tough girl. He probably wouldn't understand how someone could be this way about a towel, about a pen, about anything.

He handed me the towel.

"I just used it to dry my hair. Don't worry, I just washed it—my hair."

"Those are them too." I pointed to the pile that my mother had left at the end of his bed.

I carried the towels upstairs to my mother's room. She was sitting up in bed, with the side light on and a book in her lap, twisting her hair around her finger.

"See," I said, walking towards her, holding them like a baby in my arms, "I got my towels."

She picked up her book and began to read.

"They're mine," I said. I wanted her to tell me that she was sorry for giving my favourite towels to a guest who would just throw them on the floor, but she didn't. She didn't say anything to me; she just looked at her book.

"I walked in on them kissing," I said, and left the room.

Six

Annabel paid me one pound to wrap up her antiques in newspaper—the hand-painted teacups, a plate with a picture of the Queen on it, porcelain figures of women in wide skirts—so she could take them safely back to London.

After she was gone, my mother became very serious about not disturbing Rufus. We were quiet when we walked down the stairs and through the front hall. The whole house seemed quieter. No one else came to stay; no one even stopped by for the night.

Sometimes we would see him walk down the drive in his navy blue raincoat.

"He has a strange walk," my mother said one day. She was standing at the window watching him.

"He has a limp," I said.

He would return an hour or two later, carrying a bag of groceries from the shops. He didn't have a car.

...

This is how the autumn weeks passed: The leaves fell and fell off the trees, the mornings got darker and darker. I wore my grey

woollen tights. Eden wore his navy wool jumper. The waves got
thicker and greyer, heavier and slower.

...

On a warm day in November, my mother, Eden, and I were in
the vegetable garden. It was a small patch of earth by the shed,
where no one ever went. My mother knelt in the earth, a trowel in
her hand. There was a striped blanket with a mug of tea and a box
of biscuits on it.

Eden sat on the roots of a tree, the black-and-white cat next
to him. He wasn't ours, but sometimes he would come into our
house and Eden would give him warm milk and follow him around.

We had everything in the garden, tomatoes and lettuce and
tulips. In the summer we had strawberries; we just ate them right
there. They didn't need washing because my mother didn't use
sprays. The strawberries were gone now, and the only vegetables
left grew under the ground, carrots and turnips and potatoes.

I had my own spade to dig with. I put it in, then stepped on
it to push it farther down, but it didn't go very far. It hit a rock.
Nothing is ever easy. There were large rocks and weeds right under
the grass. This tiny patch took us months to clear. There were
worms under the rocks and black bugs that curled into tiny little
beads when you touched them. You had to be careful with the
spade, so you didn't hurt them.

"Have you seen one yet?" I asked Eden. He was looking into
a hollow cave in the tree.

"I'm not looking any more."

He had been looking for a leprechaun for two years. My mother
looked at me slowly, and I turned away.

"You look pretty today," she said. "You have roses in your
cheeks."

My socks didn't match, but I didn't care. We were all alone in the vegetable patch. My mother was wearing her beige trousers; there was dirt on her hands and knees. I went to get a biscuit but the box was empty. I looked over at Eden. He was crouched down by the bottom of the tree with twigs, moss, clover, and a pile of biscuits. I walked over quietly and stood behind him. There were four leaves lined up in a row, two big ones and two small ones; they were a family. He took the biscuits and broke them into tiny pieces and put them on a rock. It was their dinner, the leaf family.

This is where fairies and wood nymphs lived, at the base of a tree in the moss and hollows. I looked behind and saw my mother watching us, wondering what I would do. I could take all the biscuits or just step on the leaves and then pretend I hadn't seen them. "It was just a leaf," I would say. He was so quiet; everything was in his head and he looked so small, crouched at the bottom of the tree. The wind blew in, warm and soft, and took something out of me. I went back to the patch I was digging, pulling up the stones, shaking the dirt from the roots.

I heard a soft whistling. At first I thought it was the wind far away, but when I looked up I saw someone standing at the other end of the garden. It was the man in the downstairs room, Rufus. He was looking up into a tree, whistling to it. He stood very still, then a small bird flew down and landed on his head. He whistled again and the bird said something back. Then it flew off, ruffling the hair on the top of his head. He turned to watch it. Then he started walking in our direction. I don't think he saw us. He walked through the woods, and the trees were thick. I could hear him, his footsteps through the leaves.

My mother looked up. "Who's that?" she said, but she knew right away and wiped the dirt off her knees.

He saw us too and walked slowly towards us, looking up, then back down at his feet.

"Hello," my mother said. The plant she was holding fell out of her hand into the dirt.

"I was just taking a walk. I was going to have a look at the sea. I didn't mean to bother you. . . ." He looked at me and I looked away quickly.

"No, no, you're not. It must be freezing now, the sea." She laughed to herself, a nervous tickle.

"I wasn't going to swim," he said.

"Oh, I know," my mother said, bending down to pick up the plant she had dropped. I thought he would walk away, but he just stood there.

"This is a very . . . Did you do it all? By yourself?" He was looking at the garden, his arms hanging at his sides.

"May helped, and Eden. My friend Annabel told me where to plant what; she's a decorator. I would have just plopped it all down. Getting the weeds out is the hardest part. That takes the longest."

"Are there lots of stones?" he asked. "I can help. I can dig with a shovel, I think."

"You'll get all muddy. I mean your clothes. . . ."

He looked down to see what he was wearing. It was almost the same as yesterday: grey corduroy trousers and a thin navy jumper, old brown shoes.

"I don't care. I have more clothes."

"You can dig that spot. I'm trying to make it bigger." She handed him the spade. I sat on the ground and picked out the little stones with my hands. I didn't say anything. Eden was quiet, still sitting at the bottom of the tree. We stayed for a long time in the garden. Rufus dug out the edge, making it bigger. The air was warm, but the sky was turning grey above us. Occasionally, one of us would look up, wondering if it would suddenly start to rain.

Eden came over and tugged on our mother's sleeve. "I'm getting hungry," he said.

She stood up and looked over at Rufus. He was still digging with one foot on the spade. He was concentrating, really trying.

"Would you like a cup of tea?" she asked in his direction, but the wind blew her voice away. She started to walk towards him but stopped and asked again, taking a breath first. "I'm going in for a cup of tea. Would you like one?"

He turned around to face her. There was colour in his cheeks now. "Okay. I mean, yes, I would love one."

"God, you've done well with your digging," my mother said.

"I want some tea, Mum," Eden said. He was standing next to the tree, touching the bark with his fingers.

"Well, come on, then," she said, and started to walk towards the house with Rufus.

"Are you coming, May?" Eden asked me. I shook my head. I was stuck to the ground. Eden came over to where I was sitting and stood in front of me.

"Don't touch it, May. I'm not done yet." He was talking about the house he was making at the bottom of the tree.

I looked up at him.

"Please don't ruin it," he said softly, above my head. Then he looked behind him. Our mother and Rufus were nearly at the house and he ran to them, his skinny arms flapping at his side.

When they had gone into the house I pushed myself up off the ground and walked over to the tree where Eden had been playing. There were some acorns, leaves in piles, small stones and twigs: a whole world of something I couldn't see any more. When you are six years old you can sit at the bottom of a tree and everything becomes alive around you. The moss is a soft green carpet, the stone a sofa, the hollows of the tree a house.

The wind was a low voice around me. It was getting darker out. The kitchen light was on and I could see the yellow walls and the long shadows made when someone walked past the light. I stared down at the base of the tree, but all I could see was a pile of twigs and leaves and a few stones. This is how I know I'm getting older: a stick is just a stick.

Seven

Early one night there was a knock at the door. I opened it. It was Rufus.

"Hi, May," he said. "Is Lucy here?" I yelled to my mother, but she had already heard his voice and was at my side. "Do you want to go for a walk?" he asked us. She had to hold her lips together so she wouldn't smile. I think she was hoping for this, that he would walk up the stairs and knock on our door. She was always making excuses to go downstairs, to make sure the phone worked, to check the post.

The four of us had to walk across a field of sheep to get to the woods. They were asleep in bundles and ran away from us as we walked through. We were as quiet as possible; we tiptoed past them. The bravest ones stood up on their feet and made a noise at us.

"I wish we didn't have to disturb them," Rufus said.

There was another way to the woods, down the drive and past the farmer's house.

"We could have gone the other way, Mum," I said.

"I know, I'm sorry, I didn't think about the sheep." She said it like she was kicking herself.

"Don't worry, they'll go back to sleep. I didn't mean it like that. I just meant as a person, being a person, people always disturb other things. . . ." He was explaining away, moving his hand in the air, apologizing. His voice was soft and sorry; he knew how easy it was to make her stumble.

"Mum says she's always the one being bothered," Eden said, running up to take her hand. "'Mum, where's my book? Mum, where's my socks? Mum, where's my bum?'" He was skipping up and down, holding on to our mother's hand, swinging her arm. When they laughed, they looked at each other, my mother and Rufus.

"Skip with me!" Eden said, pulling her ahead. He was happy outside at night; he wasn't even scared. Rufus and I were left behind, walking together.

"I know what you mean," I said, walking closer to him so my mother wouldn't hear me. "Because once I was walking home from school and it was dark because it was winter, so I couldn't see the pavement." He leaned his face closer to hear me. I was nervous but I liked him because he seemed nervous too. My mother looked back at us and I closed my mouth. When she looked away I said, "I stepped on something and it smushed underneath my foot. I felt it, but I kept walking and didn't look at it; but I know it was a snail, and I kept thinking that it was trying to cross the road to get to its babies or that it was in love and was going to meet the other snail. And I ruined it all." I couldn't really explain it to him, the feeling of having ruined something else's life.

"That's exactly what I meant," he said to me, and lifted his head slowly so he stood straight. We walked on a little further side by side. The woods looked like a curtain in front of us. It wasn't a dark night. The sky was the colour of the sea in winter, that grey-blue. The moon was almost full, full and low.

We could see our path and each other clearly. When I looked behind us, the sheep were back together again in bundles on the short grass that they eat and sleep on. It's everything to them.

The wind blew in from the sea, which you could hear some-where out there. On the other side, the field, suddenly stopped and dropped into the water. You had to be careful on dark nights, when there was no moon, not to walk straight off the cliff. There was only a low barbed-wire fence to keep the sheep in. This was the cliff where, one night, a teenage boy left his girlfriend in a bar and took a train late at night, drunk, drunk with a heavy drowning heart, and threw himself onto the sharp and jagged rocks below. I wondered if maybe, in the middle of the air, he wished he hadn't. Don't run at night, especially in the fog.

"Why do you think the sheep never fall off?" I asked Rufus, but he didn't answer. I looked up at him to see if he heard and was thinking about it. He was looking straight ahead, at my mother and Eden.

"Sorry, what?" he asked, leaning forward again.

"Nothing."

The woods were all around us. We followed the trail that led to the wheat fields. Eden thought we were looking for the haunted house, but I had walked this path to its end and had never seen it. To the end and back takes an hour and a half; I just walked and walked. On the way home I would imagine that my father had made a surprise visit from London to see me and that he would be walking from the house, through the woods towards me. But he never was. Then it turned into a phone call, and I imagined that there would be a note on the table in my mother's handwriting that he had phoned. That's what happens to hope: it gets smaller and smaller.

Eden walked along behind Mum, swinging his arms and looking at the ground. He was holding his little black torch now that we were in the woods and it was darker. Sometimes he would start to sing a few lines of that song, the summer song, the one Jolene and I waited for on the radio. It was everywhere that summer and now it was in the middle of the woods.

"Now all the trees have heard it too," Rufus said. My mother laughed. Everything he said made her laugh.

"Look!" Eden shone the torch at something on the ground. "Look, Mum! Mum, look!" He scuffled down to his knees and looked at the spot like a squinty-eyed inspector.

"What? What is it?" she asked, kneeling down next to him. Rufus knelt down next to her to get a good look too. I just stood there. I knew Eden was just getting excited about a root or leaf or something.

They stared quietly at the spot where Eden shone the light for a few minutes until Rufus said, "What are we looking at?"

"That rock!" Eden shouted. He shone the light on a big mossy rock. "It looks like the rock that had King Arthur's sword in it!"

They moved in a little closer and huddled around the rock as though it were a tiny fire on a freezing night. There was a dent in the top and Rufus ran his finger over it. Then he looked up at my mother, keeping his hand on the rock. I saw him looking at her. The light from the torch shone on her mouth and neck and breath. When she turned to him, their eyes caught and he looked lost for a moment. Then she turned quickly towards Eden and asked, "Is it the rock?" Her voice shook. Rufus looked down and my mother turned her face back to the rock and asked, without looking at him, "What do you think?"

"It could be. It's possible. It looks like a sword was in it," Rufus told Eden.

"I really think it is. We just learned about it in school and I saw the picture and it looks just like this." Eden couldn't believe his luck; he had finally found something. It wasn't a leprechaun, it wasn't the haunted house; Eden had found King Arthur's stone.

"Wasn't it a big stone in a lake?" I said.

"Oh." Eden let out a long moan and flung his hand to his head like he was swatting a mosquito. "I forgot about the lake," he moaned.

"Well, maybe there was a lake here and it dried up. It was a long, long time ago," Rufus said. Eden filled up with air again; he came back to life instantly.

"I bet it did. It did! I knew it."

"We'll get a book from the library and find out," my mother said to him as she stood up and brushed the leaves from her clothes. We all stood up except Rufus, still on his knees. My mother held out her hand to him. He took it and she pulled him up. I saw his face wince.

"Thank you," he said, when he was standing. "I have a bad leg." He held on to her hand.

"Should we turn back?" my mother asked, looking at Rufus as their hands slid apart.

"What happened to your leg?" Eden asked, looking up at him.

"I can't remember exactly, but I hurt it when I was very young."

"Can you swim?" Eden wanted to know.

Rufus nodded.

"Can you run?"

He nodded again. "But not very fast."

"Can you ride a bike?"

"That's easy. It doesn't hurt at all."

The air was cooler now; our breath looked like thin smoke in front of us. A sound like a howl came from the trees. In the daytime you only hear the leaves beneath you, the singing birds, and, in winter, the creaking ice, but at night there are other sounds in the woods. I shivered, but not because I was cold. No one spoke. A low whispering sound came from deeper inside the woods and then a sharp cry.

"I'm getting a little tired and hungry for cheese toast," Eden said. I wanted to go home too. That's what houses are for, people at night. We turned around and walked back quietly through the woods.

...

Something woke me. A sound. It sounded like a trumpet. I thought someone was playing the trumpet downstairs. My eyes stung, they were wide open. Some people can sleep through anything.

Once I phoned my father, it was only six or seven in the evening; I was alone in the house and wanted to talk to him. A man answered the phone, but it wasn't him, it was his friend Fred, who sells pills to people—all different colours for all different things. He keeps them hidden in the hollow body of a baby doll.

Fred said, "Hold on a minute, will you?"

I waited with the phone to my ear. I waited a long time; I thought maybe we had been disconnected.

Finally someone picked up the phone. It was Fred again. "Yeah, he's knackered," he said, in his heavy, lazy voice. "He just took a sleeping pill. He's having a little lie-down on the sofa."

"Okay," I said, like it was nothing, and put the phone down. I looked at it for a moment. Everything was quiet around me. I imagined my father lying on the sofa with his feet up, not wanting to be bothered, looking at the phone, looking at his feet, a cigarette in his hand, a record on. "This is a good track," he'd say to Fred when he came back in the room, after he'd hung up the phone.

I was wide awake now, wondering if I would ever be too tired to talk to my father on the phone. Then I heard it again, the sound from downstairs. I sat up in bed. It was the middle of night and anything can happen then. Things can move around: toy animals, books, painted glass jars filled with earrings and hair clips. I've seen things happen. Once, I was lying on the top bunk—it was late and my light was on, just a bare bulb hanging in the middle of the room with a shoelace pull string—and I saw something fly across the room, slowly. A little black bird! A little black bird flew across my room and then disappeared. It really did. I saw it, and it wasn't just because I was young and thought everything was alive.

I put my feet on the floor. I was still afraid something would grab my ankle from under the bed, so I ran to the door. A grey-blue light came in through the hallway windows. As I walked down the stairs the sounds came closer; they rose up around me, like a choir. My face and chest felt warm, almost hot, as though I was sitting next to a fire.

At the bottom of the stairs, in between the crash and howl from the waves and the wind, I could hear the sounds of a school yard, a playground, a children's playground. The sound of running feet, a bell from an ice-cream van, the squeak of the swings. "Push me higher!" Young voices, high voices, boys' and girls' voices. They were coming from the yellow living room at the end of the hallway. The door was open a crack; a light was on inside. I walked towards it.

Outside the door, the air smelled of soapy warm bathwater. I put my hand on the knob and pushed it open. The light shone in my eyes, very yellow and too bright. I stepped back and put my hand above my eyes. I saw two people sitting on the floor across from a brightly coloured board game. A boy and a girl, younger than me but older than Eden. They were wearing their school uniforms. I closed my eyes and saw red. The next time I opened them the light was calmer. My mother and Rufus sat on the floor across from each other playing a game of Scrabble.

My mother was laughing. She was really laughing, bending over at the waist. Rufus looked at me as I stood in the doorway. "She keeps trying to add two 'eds' to everything," he said. He was laughing too; his eyes were bright.

"It's the double past!" she said, her eyes shiny and her cheeks red. She looked like a girl.

"Did we wake you?" my mother asked. She looked like she was about to start laughing again. I didn't answer because I wasn't sure. I sat down on the sofa and pulled my legs to my chest. There was a folded plaid blanket on the arm of the sofa; I put it over my feet and lay down. A fire was burning low in the fireplace. There was a record playing. I closed my eyes and listened for the trumpet.

I was almost asleep when I heard Rufus say in a low voice, "Why did you leave him?"

"What?" my mother asked, as though she hadn't heard.

"Their father," he said.

"They have different fathers. May's father is Simon. Eden's father was Paul. I left Simon because I wasn't in love with him. I don't think he was really in love with me. We were both young; I was twenty when I had May. There was no love lost, as Annabel would say."

"Who's Paul?" Rufus asked. His voice sounded stiff.

"An old boyfriend. . . . May thought he was always drunk, but he was high." She sounded like she was talking to an old friend, Annabel or Suzy. Her voice didn't change when she spoke to him, the way it sometimes did with men.

I wanted her to talk about my father, not Eden's.

"I got pregnant. I didn't want to have another child."

When she said things like that, that she didn't want another child, I didn't know what to think of myself.

"I went to stay with my friend Suzy in her mother's house in Somerset," she told him. "She had two big dogs, and May used to follow them into the woods by herself. We'd be so stoned we wouldn't even notice. Then when we did I'd be in a huge panic and run around to all the neighbours and phone the police.

Everyone would be looking for her. Once, I was sure I'd lost her, she was gone for three hours, but then someone found her walking down the road with one of the dogs."

My mother's voice sounded slow and loose, like beads on a necklace with a string that's too long.

"Anyway Suzy drove me to the clinic, and May sat in the back seat."

I remembered sitting in the back of the car. No one would tell me where we were going. The trees were all bare bones and the sky was white, it was that kind of winter day. I was different then. I would sit on my mother's lap and put my head on her chest; inside me was just me and warm blue water.

I pulled the blanket up slowly, over my face, so Rufus and my mother couldn't see that I was listening. When I remembered being little, in the back of that car, it made me feel like I missed someone.

My mother was still telling him the story.

"On the way, Suzy pointed to the side of the road and said, 'Did you see that dead deer?' Then May said, 'Where's the dead deer? Where's the dead deer?'"

She was imitating my voice, the way it used to sound, small and high.

"She was looking all over for the deer. I told her that we had already passed it, but she kept turning around trying to see it. 'Dead deer? Dead deer? Where's the dead deer?' she kept saying the whole drive. We tried to play I Spy and asked her if she wanted an ice lolly, but she wouldn't stop asking about the dead deer. . . . There was something about the way she kept saying 'dead deer', over and over, that made me change my mind."

It was my fault Eden was born.

"Does Eden ever see him?"

"Paul? No, he didn't want to have a child. Eden never even asks about him," my mother said.

I was waiting for her to tell him about my father.

But the next time she spoke she said, "It's your go."

"My letters are terrible. Where's May's father?"

"In London somewhere . . . ." I was wide awake with the blanket over my face. I opened my eyes. I thought I would be able to hear better. Then the record ended and the next thing she said was, "What should we listen to?"

I heard her stand up and lift the needle; it made a scratchy sound. No one spoke for a while. Then she said, "I'm getting tired."

"Do you want me to take her upstairs?" I heard him ask.

"No, she's fine." I felt my mother pull the blanket down to cover my feet; then she slowly lifted it off my face. She didn't want me to suffocate in the night.

They turned the lights out and left. I heard him say good night to her in the hallway, and I heard them walk away from each other.

I lay there in the dark, on the sofa, with the plaid blanket over me. I felt like I was sinking to sleep. Then I heard someone walk into the room, quietly. I held my breath, I could hear breathing, close to me. I opened my eyes and waited for the dark to turn a lighter grey. I saw someone, a body, lying down on the floor next to the sofa.

"Mum?"

"Yes."

"What are you doing?"

"I'm just thinking, don't worry." Her voice sounded like it was sailing off somewhere.

I fell asleep that way, in the living room, in the middle of the night, while my mother slept below me, on the floor, in the place where Rufus had been before.

Eight

The next morning the phone woke me. I sat up in bed, waiting, listening for my mother or Eden to pick it up. It rang and rang, the precious phone. Anyone could be on the other end, even my father. I ran to it with a swooping hope that he wouldn't get bored and put it down. It was Sunday! Sometimes he calls on Sunday, I thought, as I reached for it.

I took a breath before I answered.

"Hello," I said. The line was empty, but I could still hear the phone ringing. It was the pay phone. I ran downstairs. I felt a splinter in the bottom of my foot, but I didn't stop. I kept running towards it.

"Hello?" I stood on one foot.

"Is Rufus in?" a woman asked from the other end.

"Hold on," I said. I put the phone down on the table. This is how hope falls away. I walked on my toes. The floor was cold, and the splinter stung in my foot. The house suddenly seemed so big, it made me tired thinking about looking for him in it. My heart was still beating fast. I went down to the cellar and knocked on his door. There was no answer. I called his name through the hallways, but there was still no answer.

I walked upstairs to the guest sitting room, the yellow room. The Scrabble game was still on the floor; next to it lay a piece of paper with their names, Lucy and Rufus; below were their scores. The plaid blanket lay crumpled at the end of the sofa. I remembered that I had come into this room last night and fallen asleep on the sofa. I thought, How did I get back to my own room? When I tried to remember, it all seemed so far away. I shouted my mother's name, but no one heard me; my voice didn't carry. I wondered what time it was. I yelled my brother's name from the bottom of the stairs. I felt so tired and my foot hurt. I was being slow on purpose, looking out of the window, letting her wait on the other end of the phone. Making her sit and wait with the phone against her ear. I walked back slowly.

"He's not here," I said. The phone felt heavy in my hand. I looked around at the dark wood, the archway over the door, and thought, I'm alone in this house.

"What do you mean?" she asked when I told her. I had heard her voice before, it was someone I knew. "He doesn't have a car. He can't go anywhere. Is this May?"

"Yes."

"It's Patricia."

"Oh, hi," I said. I was happy she remembered my name.

"I'm calling from London. I have to ask him something. Is your mother there?" I wondered if maybe she knew my father. I wanted to ask her but she sounded like she was in a rush.

"I think she went out." It is what I really thought. She could have been asleep; I still didn't know what time it was.

"Is he with her?"

"Who?"

"Rufus," she said.

"Do you know what time it is?" I thought it might be so early that everyone was still asleep. I looked up at the sky through the windows—it was a heavy blue, the way it sometimes is in the early morning before it brightens up.

"It's half past eleven," she said impatiently. "Did they go out together?"

"I don't know." I was thinking about how late it was and wondering how I had slept through everyone waking up, eating breakfast, getting dressed.

It seemed like a long time passed. Neither of us spoke.

"May?" Her voice sounded higher, softer. "Will you do me a favour?"

"What?" I thought she was going to ask me to write down a long message on a piece of paper.

"Don't tell him I phoned. Okay?"

"Don't tell him you phoned?" I repeated it to make sure.

"Do not tell him."

"Okay." I was nervous that I would forget and tell him anyway.

"I'll bring you something from London, a little surprise. When I come to visit," she said, and put the phone down.

I was excited for a moment, thinking about what she would bring me from London. I liked small things, little surprises. Once in my Christmas stocking there was what looked like a chocolate in its own clear box. But it was made of plastic, the top twisted off, and inside was a pool of raspberry-coloured lip gloss. I hoped she would bring me something like that.

There was a note on the kitchen table. It was in my mother's terrible handwriting that I could barely read.

Gone shopping, but will be back soon to make you fluffy pancakes for breakfast.

Love,
Mummy

A damp wind came in through the half-opened window. It felt like it was raining outside, but it wasn't; it was just Sunday. I sat down on one of the kitchen chairs and looked at the bottom of my foot. There was a splinter in my heel, a small spot of blood; it was easy to pull out. Everything was so quiet in the house. I wondered if my mother had tried to wake me up this morning.

I went to my bedroom. I looked in the mirror and practised ballet. I made up my own moves. Sometimes I wore a scarf around my head and pretended it was long hair. I brushed my hair with my blue hairbrush, starting at the ends so it didn't hurt. It came just below my shoulders, a dirty-blonde colour. I turned to look at myself from the side. I lifted my shirt to see my stomach. It looked flat, but when I sat down there were rolls. I saw my French book lying on the floor and sneered at it. I was three lessons behind, pages and pages behind. I felt cold and went to run a bath.

After the bath I put on a T-shirt and then a sweatshirt, clean polka-dot knickers that went up to my waist, blue trousers, and clean socks. My skin was pink and I felt warm and new again. Then I went to the window to see if my mother's car was coming down the driveway. My stomach growled; I looked down at it. My wet hair made a puddle in the middle of my back. I thought, I shouldn't start my French lessons yet because they will be back soon and I'll have to stop in the middle.

I sat on my bed and waited. I thought about different kinds of foods: a pink strawberry mousse swirling in a wineglass, cheese on toast. I walked to the kitchen. I thought about eating a bowl of cereal but decided to wait. They would be home soon and then we'd have fluffy pancakes. The reason fluffy pancakes are fluffy is because you have to whip the egg whites separately until they are stiff and then carefully fold them into the batter—very carefully. Our mother always does that part. When they're done we keep them warm in the oven; then we cover them with butter and the maple syrup that my grandmother sends us from America. Sometimes we use strawberry jam.

I thought I heard a car coming, but it was just the wind blowing through the leaves. I read the note from my mother again. I looked at the clock; it was almost one. All I could feel was my stomach sinking and sinking. I decided to make a list of what to eat that day. The first thing was fluffy pancakes with maple syrup and butter. That's all I wrote; it was a boring thing to do. I stood up and felt dizzy. I put my hands on my stomach. It wasn't as flat as it felt.

I went back to my room; I thought it would be warmer in there. When I stood up my head felt like it dropped down. A bump, a bump in my head. I picked up my French workbook: *le cahier, le musée, la rose, la chienne*. I couldn't stand it, the sound of the language. I liked my own. I held out my hand in front of me. It looked white; I thought maybe there was no blood in it. I wasn't sure if I was hungry any more; things kept disappearing around me. I found a clock and it was quarter to two. They must have had a flat tyre. I counted the hours since I last ate. Almost twenty.

I walked to the kitchen. I looked at the phone; it just sat there and looked back at me. I opened the refrigerator; everything looked cold. I went to my mother's room. She hadn't made her bed yet, blankets and pillows and baby pillows all piled up. I got in it and pulled the pile over me. I thought about eating some cereal, but it seemed cold and terrible to me. Toast, biscuits, baked beans, the leftover onion soup—but all I wanted was those fluffy pancakes. I thought I heard a car, I jumped up and ran over to the window. My toes were freezing, I pressed my face to the glass and held my breath, but there was no car. Soon, I thought. They'll be home soon.

Waiting is the longest feeling. I went back to the kitchen.

Finally I really did hear a car coming up the driveway. I stood up out of my mother's bed. It was almost three. I heard voices:

my mother's, Rufus's, Eden's. The rustling sound of bags, doors opening and closing. They had all gone out together, and they hadn't even tried to wake me.

"You slept late this morning," my mother said. She walked in with fresh air and sun around her. Rufus came in behind her, carrying shopping bags. They didn't look hungry.

"Hello. You slept late?" Rufus said to me.

I stood there like a storm. He put the bags down on the table and started unloading them.

"Did you get your schoolwork done?" my mother asked. I watched her put the car keys on the table.

"I'm hungry," I said to the ground.

"Didn't you eat anything?" She looked concerned. I thought maybe it was an old note I had found lying on the table this morning.

"Mum bought me a doughnut!" Eden said, leaning against the wall, his hands behind his back. I could see the sugar around his mouth. I thought, He's never been as hungry as I am right now.

"I thought you were going to make fluffy pancakes."

She looked at me, and her hand went to her mouth. "Oh, no. We forgot to get eggs from the egg woman." She stood like that with her hand on her mouth and her eyes wide. "I'm so sorry, darling. Oh, God, I knew I was forgetting something."

I was trying to remember if I ever forgot things.

"You haven't eaten anything at all today?"

I shook my head. "You said in the note that you were coming back soon. I was waiting for you." I wished I hadn't said that. I didn't want her to know I had waited for her.

Eden and Rufus were both looking at me. The room was quiet; I had been whining.

"Darling, I'll make you lunch." She walked over to me and stroked my hair. I looked at the floor.

"I brought you back something." She pulled out a pink-and-white-striped paper bag. It was from the pastry shop in Sheperton, the town. That's where they had gone; it was almost like a city. She handed me the bag. "Don't eat it yet," she said. "I'll make you some proper food first."

"Lucy, where does this go?" Rufus asked, holding out a box of Familia.

My mother turned to him. "Just up there," she said, pointing to the cupboard. She watched him for a moment, and then she looked back at me.

Rufus was opening cupboards behind her. I thought, Why is he putting food away in someone else's kitchen? Doesn't he have a book to write?

"What is it? What is it?" Eden ran towards me to look. He held his own pink-and-white bag in his hand.

My mother stood next to me—she put her hands on my shoulders—and Eden stood in front of me, waiting to see what I had from the pastry shop. It was all the attention I ever wanted this morning, but it was too late. I opened the bag; the smell was warm and lemony. Inside were two fairy cakes wrapped up in rose-tinted wax paper. I put my hand in the bag and lifted one of them out. I unwrapped the wax paper; it was a tiny square cake with yellow icing and little painted pink-and-white flowers on it. I just wanted to look at it. It was doll-like and precious.

I thought of them at the pastry shop in town, where there were people sitting at round white tables drinking cups of tea and coffee and eating cakes. I wanted to turn around and kick my mother, but I was so tired I felt like I might fall over. I wanted her to take me and sit me down in the chair and spoon-feed me.

"I had some cappuccino," Eden said to me.

"One sip," my mother said. She gave him a look that said, Be quiet; don't tell her what we did this afternoon. The fairy cake was in the palm of my hand. I tasted the icing, a tiny bit on my finger, then sweet and stinging on the tip of my tongue. I looked at the cake in my hand. Then I let it drop to the floor.

...

There was a soft knock on the door. I rolled over on my side facing the wall. Turning away is so easy: a turn of the head, an unanswered question, an unreturned phone call, a letter thrown in a pile. My mother opened the door and came in. I heard her walking towards me, slowly, looking at the floor to make sure she didn't step on anything. I felt her put her hand on my shoulder, and the side of the bed sank a little as she sat down on it. I opened my eyes halfway. The room was a shadowy dark. It smelled like toast; she was bringing me food. I couldn't wait for today to be over.

My mother sat next to me on the bed. I could hear her breathing. Then I felt her hand in my hair, and that place behind my ribs ached and my shoulders began to shake. Then I was crying.

"What's the matter?"

Her hand rested on my forehead. I couldn't catch my breath, I was almost choking. I didn't think I would be able to talk; my throat felt sore. She turned her body to me and I put my face in the sheets.

"Try to tell me, please."

She stroked my hair again, and this made me calmer. I wanted to just fall asleep, but my head hurt and my eyes stung.

"Why do you get so angry with me?"

This made me start again from my stomach. I didn't want her to think there was something wrong with me. She never saw what I was really like. The other day when I was alone, walking home from school, eating the packet of crisps the man in the shop gave me, I felt so calm and light. I walked down the quiet road singing a song to myself. I thought, Yes, this is the way I was born. This is the way I am; I'll be able to dance in front of my mother, to wrap my arms around her; I'll tell her everything. But then something turns, like a splinter in my chest, and I'm me again, frowning at the ground. That's what I wanted to tell her, but it's hard to scrape the truth out of your chest.

I looked outside at the trees. They said, It's hard, it's hard.

I took a breath—it was loud and shaky—and said, "You're mean to me on purpose." I was on my side facing away from her.

"May, I would never try to be mean to you."

"You always tell your friends bad things about me. I heard you. You said, 'May is difficult.' You said it to Suzy on the phone and to Granny." My voice got louder and louder, like a flame.

"You *can* be difficult. I also say how wonderful you are. I'm sorry if that hurt you. I love you." She said that as though it would make up for everything: *I love you*, the biggest gift of all. *I love you* meant nothing to me; it wasn't like a ten-pound note falling out of a birthday card.

"Why didn't you come back and make fluffy pancakes like you said you would?"

"I forgot, darling. I'm sorry, I really forgot. Anyway, you usually like to be left alone." She put her hand on my shoulder. We were quiet for a long time. It was almost dark out now. I could see the trees from my window, against the sky.

My mother said, "I made you a cheese-and-tomato sandwich." I sat up and pulled my knees to my chest. The sandwich was on her lap in a saucer.

"May, you should try to tell me when you're upset with me. You have to talk about things." She ran her hand down my back.

"Please send me to live with my father." I let my hand fall against the mattress. I thought, I'll just start over, find someone new: my father.

"You don't even know him," my mother said.

Then she was quiet, her hand still on my back.

"I can help you," my mother said. "You get yourself in such a state about these things."

I wanted help, I wanted to be pulled to the shore. I looked down at my hands. I felt calmer now.

"Do you want some mint tea with milk?"

I nodded. She leaned towards me and kissed the top of my head. When she left, a slant of light came through the door, but nothing changed. Next to me the cheese-and-tomato sandwich sat on the blue-and-white saucer. I looked at it and thought, I don't really need to eat at all. Knowing that was like a piece of magic, a gift, like being able to fly. But my bones and skin felt itchy and thirsty, and my stomach felt like it was somewhere else far away. I don't need to eat, I'm not grabbing the sandwich; I'll just take a bite slowly, a small bite, a baby bite.

When I stood up holding the empty saucer with only crumbs and a piece of crust left, I felt more like me again. All one thing.

Nine

We had a surprise test in French class. Madame Monet, our teacher, wrote down three questions on the blackboard for us to answer.

"Only three! That's all, girls." She lifted her arms in the air as if to say, See, it's nothing, as light as air. Her straight dark hair was pulled tightly off her face in a small bun, her eyes done with dark liner, and her lips the shape of a kiss. There was something about the way she moved that made me think of a marionette.

I stared at the three questions on the board. I saw her look at me and I bent down over a piece of paper, but all I wrote was my name. I saw Jolene across the room, hunched over her desk.

When Madame Monet turned her back, the heads of three girls in front of me, Barbara, Courtney and Polly, came together as quick as a pull-string purse. Barbara's hair fell straight and sunny over the back of her chair. I could see them showing each other the answers. The three of them were on each other's side. On the floor by the side of Barbara's desk was a red plastic heart-shaped handbag. Soon all the girls will have one, I thought.

When I got home, I went to my room and sat at my desk with my *cahier* in front of me. Today, I said, I'll start; from now on. . . .

I looked and looked at the book, and every time I lifted my head it was darker outside. It made me nervous the way time did that, the empty notebook pages, the black lines to fill in. I stood up and pushed the notebook off my desk, and then I stood in the middle of my room. Outside, the trees looked in at me, and I saw a girl throw her book against the wall.

My mother and Eden were in our small sitting room with the sloped ceiling and tiny square fireplace. This was meant for one person, one woman, the headmistress of the school. They never had husbands or children of their own, just a small dog, a Scottie with a tartan raincoat. I imagined her by the window, in her favourite cushioned chair, at a round table, a blanket on her lap with a book and a tea tray. She would sit under a circle of light from the standing lamp with the flower-shaped shade.

Downstairs the schoolgirls would be in their nightgowns, plain white cotton ones, talking in bed, giggling, getting up, sneaking to the kitchen. That was long ago when this house was a happy school. I think I've seen them in the middle of the night, wandering down the hallways, disappearing around the corners like the thinnest part of the moon.

Eden was on the sofa, wrapped in a big white towel. His hair was wet and sticking up all over the place. He looked like a duck.

"You look like a duck," I said.

My mother looked up at me. She was sitting in the big green chair, an old heavy red leather book open on her lap. It was a photo album, one I had never seen before.

"What are you doing?"

"I'm just looking for something." She was turning the pages slowly, concentrating. The photographs were yellowing, black and white squares falling down the pages. I stood with my arms crossed in front of me.

"Come here." She patted her leg. I walked over, dragging my feet, and sat down on the arm of the chair.

"I want to go somewhere." I wasn't sure how to act, I felt half melted. I thought she wanted me to be like him, my brother. 'Easy'; that's how I've heard her describe him to her friends. Eden looked at me and looked away like he knew something, a secret about me.

"What, darling?" she asked, staring at the photos.

"I want to go for a ride in the car somewhere." A drive, a drive. I thought if we drove away everything would be different when we returned. It's like when you can't find something, you have to leave the room for a while so it can work, the magic. Go outside and count to ten, walk up and down the stairs, turn around in circles, and then when you come back it will be there, easy to find. Now it was a drive, and then I thought I would come back and be able to do my French homework.

"Let's get ice cream from the special place, the little place with the balloons," Eden said, walking towards us with his towel open.

"I can see your ugly little willy," I said.

He turned around quickly and wrapped the towel tighter. My mother poked her elbow in my side.

"Don't, you'll make him self-conscious."

But nothing had changed about him. He turned right back around and said, "Mum, remember the man that gave me the balloon that floated, and I got the chocolate ice cream with marshmallows?"

My mother nodded and said, "Then you got sick."

"That's because you made me eat fish!" Eden said.

She turned another page and looked across the room. "Okay. Let's take a drive there."

We all stood up, then my mother looked around suddenly and said, in a hushed voice, "Eden, go downstairs and ask Rufus if he wants to come with us."

"Okay." He turned to run out; he loved to have a mission.

"Wait!" she yelled. "Don't say I told you to ask, just act as if we were wondering."

He nodded and wrapped his towel around him like a cape. He pattered down the hallway and then down the stairs. It was quiet, just the two of us.

Her face changed; suddenly, she looked worried. "I hope we're not bothering him."

She sat down and waited, twisting her hair around her finger. Her legs moved up and down under her skirt. Girls in my class did this, shook their legs. I had never seen my mother do it before; it bothered me. I sat down and pointed my toes, then flexed them, then pointed them, an exercise we do in gym. But I did it to have something else to do, to show I didn't care if he came with us or not.

A few minutes later we heard Eden running up the stairs, making aeroplane noises. He ran into the room, red-faced, catching his breath, holding the towel around his shoulders with one hand. In the other he held a small folded white piece of paper which he handed to my mother. It read, *I would love to go out for ice cream with you.*

My mother stood up. "That means he wants to come, right?"

"Yes," we both said together, because sometimes we couldn't believe her questions. It was as if she didn't understand words clearly.

"Okay. He's coming, good." She took a deep breath and walked over to the mirror, looked at it, then walked away.

"Did he say he would come up here?"

Eden shrugged.

"Where's the pen? Where's the pen?" She sounded panicky, as though she were saying, "There's a fire, there's a fire!" There were two pencils on the table by her chair in an old mustard jar.

She tore a corner from the old newspaper on the table and wrote, *We'll be ready in ten minutes. Let's meet by the front door.*

She folded the note and wrote his name on it.

Eden stuck his arm out straight, a messenger to the Queen. My mother put the note on the palm of his hand and he closed his fingers round it. Then he pedalled his bare little feet, running in place, making aeroplane noises, then he flung out his arms, using the towel for wings. I hoped he'd get a splinter too.

I saw my mother walk over to the mirror again. Then she put her hand on top of her head and said, "I shouldn't have written that. I should have just knocked on his door."

I followed her to the bathroom. She splashed some water on her face, looked in the mirror, pulled her hair out of the ponytail, brushed it down, looked again, then put it back in a ponytail. Her hands scurried in the bottom of her handbag for a lipstick. When she pulled it out, the lid was missing and there were little pieces of tobacco and things stuck on it. She wiped the top off with a piece of toilet paper and dabbed it on her lips.

"Why are you putting that on?"

She looked at me blankly. I put my hands in my back pockets and stared back at her.

"Patricia's his girlfriend, you know," I said.

She wiped the colour from her lips with the back of her hand and pushed past me. "What am I doing?" I heard her say, as she walked down the hallway.

"Mum! Mum, where are you? I have an urgent delivery!" Eden yelled. He bumped into my mother, spun around, and handed her another note, a corner of a plain white piece of paper, folded, with her name written on the front. She unfolded it and started to read, but the letters looked like stitching; the words meant nothing to us.

"It's written in another language," she said. Her voice was slow, skating over the ice. "Eden, hurry and get ready. May, put your coat on."

When I came back with my coat she was still looking at the note, as though it would solve itself.

"I hope it doesn't mean something bad. I mean, I hope it's not something mean."

...

Rufus was standing by the front door when we came down the stairs. His shoulders hung forward, like a shy boy's. He wasn't like other men; he didn't walk around as though he had medals pinned to his chest.

"Hello," my mother said. It came out in a nervous laugh. "Did you get a lot of work done today?"

"Some." He looked at my mother as though he was seeing her for the first time.

"What did that note mean?" she asked.

"Oh . . . nothing, really." I saw his face flush. He turned around and walked out of the door, leaving us alone in the hall. My mother stopped for a moment. She was thinking, What did I just say to make him leave? She hadn't seen the way he had looked at her because she had been watching Eden tie his shoe.

Outside was a purply dark. The wind blew in with ice on the tips of its wings. When it stopped, and the leaves settled and didn't rattle and fall, the air felt warm. Each wind brought winter closer.

My mother looked through her handbag for the car keys.

"I want the front seat!" Eden said.

"Rufus is sitting in the front seat, Eden," my mother said.

"That's all right, let him sit in front." Rufus said it so quickly and sounded so eager that I knew my mother was thinking he didn't want to sit next to her.

"Are you sure?" she asked.

"Yes," he said.

"Maybe you should just drive them. I'll stay here." She held the keys in her hand. Eden and I were used to this, her changing her mind at the last minute, deciding not to, taking it back.

"What?" Rufus asked, looking at her. Eden and I looked at him the way you look at a child who suddenly says their first word. My mother stopped, looking at him as though she were caught. What could she have said? *Because I looked in the mirror, because you walked out the door when I smiled at you, because you don't want to sit next to me, every little thing pricks me, every little thing pricks.*

"I don't know," she said, tossing the keys in her hand, trying to smile, to laugh it off. "I thought maybe . . . I want to read my book."

"You want to read instead?" It sounded like the beginning of an argument. I thought, We just need to get in the car. I stood with my hand on the side window.

"I want to go, Mum. I want ice cream," Eden said.

Our car was green and rusting around the edges. Bumping, and noisily, we drove along. Rufus sat next to me in the back, his knees squashed against the front seat. My mother turned the radio on. No one spoke. Together for the first time, we were all shy. This happens between people, suddenly, but if you stay together it ends eventually; it just passes away. I leaned my head back against the seat, the way I have seen women do in the movies, when a man kisses their neck and they slowly smile.

Usually I have to stare out at the road to make sure we don't crash. I never sleep in the car. But that night I didn't worry. I felt tired and washed out. I thought, If everything ends tonight, it will be all right. I turned my head and looked out of the window.

Eden started talking about what kind of ice lolly he was going to buy when we got to the shop. He knew all the names and prices by heart, like the times tables. The songs on the radio were new; the summer songs were over.

"The Milk Maid lolly is only twenty pence, so if I pick that I should be allowed to get two." He was serious, working it out. "Right, Mum?" Then he turned around to face us in the back seat. "What kind are you going to have?"

"I don't know," Rufus said. "What do you think?"

Eden squeezed his face together, thinking hard. "Do you like chocolate?"

Rufus nodded.

"And banana?"

Rufus nodded again.

"Then you should get the Gunky Monkey."

"The Gunky Monkey?" Rufus asked, sounding out the name.

"Doesn't cold food hurt your teeth?" That was my mother, looking straight ahead at the road.

"What?" Rufus asked, leaning forward. "Hurt my teeth?" He put his hand on the back of her seat.

"Does it sting your teeth?" Eden asked, looking through the space between the two front seats.

"Did I tell you that?" Rufus asked. Something in his voice made me nervous, and I sat up with my arms right at my sides and pulled my seat belt round me.

"What?" My mother turned her head to face him.

"Look at the road!" My voice sounded like a trap. She was always moving around while she drove: looking for something, smoking, eating just like she would in a house. I sat up so I could see the road clearly out of the front window, to be sure we were safe.

"Did I tell you that?" he asked again, but louder. She leaned sideways so her ear stuck out from behind the car seat.

That song came on the radio, the popular one from the summer.

"I like this song!" Eden said, and sang along with the wrong words.

"Tell me what?" she asked, almost turning around but then remembering.

"That cold things hurt my teeth." He said it louder, trying to make her understand, the way you speak to someone who doesn't speak your language.

"Do they?" she asked.

"No," he said. "Not any more. That was only when I was really young. Cold things haven't hurt my teeth since I was nine."

"Oh." She sounded lost.

"It's just funny," Rufus said, "I had completely forgotten about that until you reminded me." He sounded soft and happy.

The sky turned a darker blue outside. Cars drove past. Just ahead of us shone the lights from the shop windows.

...

The phone was ringing when we got home. A dull ring, not panicky, just ringing and ringing as though it had been all night. The downstairs phone, the one in the front hall for the guests.

My mother picked it up. "Hello?" she said. "Hello?" She waited, with her hand on her hip. "No one's there," she said, and put the phone down.

I walked upstairs. Eden carried the bag with the ice lollies. The only place that had been open was the little shop by the petrol station. And we bought a whole collection of them—ones we'd never tried before, with strawberry sprinkles, a mint-flavoured one, and one like a rocket.

The phone started to ring again; it was coming from our flat upstairs. I ran up the narrow wooden stairs, leaving Eden far behind me. I picked it up in the living room. "Hello?" I was out of breath.

"May?"

"Yes?"

"It's me," said the voice at the other end cheerfully.

"Hi," I said slowly. I didn't know who I was speaking to.

"Where are they?" Then I knew it was her: Patricia.

"What?"

"It's strange he hasn't phoned me, considering everything that's happened between us." She paused for a moment and took in a breath. It sounded like she was smoking. "I think they're having an affair."

I could hear my mother, Rufus and Eden coming up the stairs, their voices and footsteps. I could even hear the crinkling sound of the plastic bag with the ice lollies in it.

I pushed the phone closer to my mouth and walked to the far corner of the room, where the ceiling slants. I didn't want anyone to hear me. I opened my mouth, but I couldn't speak.

"I think your mother is trying to seduce him." I had heard that word before. I knew what it meant, but it had never been this close to me. I wondered if my mother was trying to seduce him right now, as they walked up the stairs. Seduce. I hated that word. It made me think of heavy breathing and knickers on the floor by the bed.

"Well?"

"She's married to my father!" I almost yelled it at her.

"She's married?"

"Yes. To my father, who works in London. He's a business-man." That's what I told people. That my father was a business-man—a dark suit on a hanger, a taxi back from the airport with a present in his suitcase for me, a little doll from the place he had just been. I have one, a Danish girl with long pigtails and wooden clogs, but it was from my grandmother.

"Oh." She sounded like she was trying to figure something out. "Then if they *are* having an affair, that's very serious; that's illegal. She could go to jail for it. That's adultery." She sounded strict, like a teacher.

...

Once, in London, my mother came home and told me she had been fired from her job. I thought it meant they were going to set her on fire. And now this word, "adultery"; it sounded like a type of torture. I thought about my mother in prison just waiting there, forever and ever.

I would go and visit her in the afternoons, after school. When I saw her through the bars, sitting on a metal bed. I wouldn't feel sorry for her, and I wouldn't be able to be nice. I would get angry and hate her for being stuck in there.

...

"Do they sleep in the same room?" Patricia asked, as though what she had just said was nothing important, as though she were asking for the time while she was waiting for a lift with her hand on the button. But I couldn't answer. If I opened my mouth to speak my voice would tremble, so I hung up.

I walked to my room, quickly and quietly, past the kitchen. I could hear my mother, Rufus and Eden putting bowls on the table, opening the drawer, taking out spoons. My bedroom didn't have a lock on the door and I needed to cry. I went to the bathroom and turned the lock; then I ran the water. I sat down on the floor next to the sink and opened my mouth to scream, but there was no sound: My stomach shook, and my face got hot. It was the way I cried.

Ten

I watched them, my mother and Rufus. They took long walks around the house and disappeared into the woods or to the rocks below. Walking side by side, shoulder to shoulder, their fingers nearly touching. Once, while they walked, he put his hand on the small of her back, softly, the way a leaf falls. That was the only time I ever saw them touch.

He would always look at her, wherever she was; whoever else was in the room, his eyes would go to her. If she looked up and caught him, he would move his eyes away quickly. Too quickly.

Once Eden asked, "Did you have a dog when you were little?" Eden wanted one, a dog. Rufus said yes. "What was his name? Give me a hint!" Eden loved guessing games; he was a good guesser.

But then my mother said, "Caligula?"

"What did you just say?" Rufus asked.

"That's not fair, he told you that." Eden slammed his arm down in the air.

"Was I right?" my mother asked. She looked surprised.

"I promise I didn't tell her. Did I?"

She knew things about him.

...

When Suzy phoned from London and asked questions like "What's he like in the sack?" or "Have you done it yet?" my mother looked embarrassed and said quietly into the phone, "It's not like that between us." She would try and explain. "No, he's not a poofter, I don't think so, anyway. . . . Yes, he's handsome." Then she'd try to talk about something else, Suzy's boyfriends.

"So what's going on with that idiot David?" my mother asked one day, the phone between her ear and shoulder, while she tidied the counter. Then she was quiet and listened for twenty-seven minutes—I watched the clock—while Suzy told her all about David and also Peter, another one she liked. My mother seemed a little bored and would put the phone down on the counter for a moment, while she dried a dish, then pick it back up and say, "Really?"

And I know that when something which used to be interesting—like dolls or Saturday morning telly—begins to be boring, it means you're growing up.

...

One night I left my bedroom and went looking for my mother. When I was younger, some nights I woke up with a start. I had nightmares and would get into her bed. She would wrap her arms around me and I'd fall asleep again. I didn't like to be touched like that any more, it made me feel too hot.

I walked down the dark hallway, dragging my hand lightly against the wall. My mother slept with her door open for Eden when he had nightmares. I stopped next to the door and listened. I could hear her breathing. Sometimes I wasn't sure if it was her or me, so I held my breath and looked inside. There was a cold breeze; she slept with the windows open, like my grandmother. I stared into the room. The air was dark and wavy. I couldn't see clearly. The lighthouse beacon shone in through the windows, then out again, like a circle. I thought about the man in the lighthouse on the rocks, sitting by the small window, staring out, making sure no ships sailed into each other.

Everything turned fuzzy in front of me, I saw little things in the air—dragonflies, and fairies with wings that flew across the room quickly—but I wasn't afraid. I knew it was just the dark. I stared and stared into the room; my toes got cold, but I stood there until I knew she was asleep on the bed. Just one person, just her. And then it was safe to sleep. There was no adultery in this house, it wouldn't burn down, we were safe tonight, and I could go back to my own room.

But one night she wasn't there. I didn't know what time it was. I went to the kitchen, the bathroom, the yellow sitting room downstairs. Everywhere was quiet. Where was she? I walked around in the dark, my shoulders bumping against doorways. I couldn't see anything. There was no light from outside, no moon. I was wearing my old white nightgown that was too short in the arms. I'd had it since I was ten. I felt like a child in it.

I went back into my room, turned the light on, and sat down at the end of my bed. My school satchel was on the floor. I hadn't taken anything out, I hadn't done any of my homework that night. In it was a note from my French teacher telling my mother I was "distracted" in class and seemed "irritable". My accent was "dreadful" and so was my spelling. Maybe it was a simple problem. Had I seen an optician lately?

I stood up and kicked the bag. Then I kicked it again. My stomach hurt; I wanted mint tea with milk. Where was she? I thought, What if I never see her again? Maybe she just disappeared; some people do. Then I thought about the baby elephants in Africa whose mothers were killed for their tusks. I'd seen it on the telly. The orphaned babies went crazy. When they turned into teenagers they were furious and broke things with their heads. I wanted to kill the people who had killed the elephants. I concentrated on them dying, getting sick and dying. I pulled the quilt off my bed and threw it on the floor, I made a sound like a moan and fell down on top of it.

I stood up and walked to the door. I was on my way to Rufus's room to see if my mother was there. But suddenly I felt embarrassed and sat back down on the crumpled quilt. The towels, the Bloomingdale's towels, were on my chair, folded the long way. I'll pretend I'm giving them back, I thought. I picked them up and held them like a baby in my arms. I'd say, "Here are the towels. I was just coming down here to give them to you." I put a shirt on over my nightgown. I checked my mother's room once more. I went in and felt the bed; it was flat, still made. I thought, What if I find them in his bed, naked? I made a face and walked down the stairs.

His door was closed. Light was coming under the bottom and there was a noise: a *click-click* sound. I stood outside and listened for a moment. The stone floor was freezing; the draught made my eyes cold. I knocked.

He opened the door and looked down at me, at the top of my head. I looked up at him.

"Hello, May." He sounded happy. He was wearing his regular clothes: a navy blue sweater, brown trousers and grey socks.

"Here, I just wanted to give these towels back to you." They were in my arms, an offering.

"Is something the matter?"

I looked past him into the room. She wasn't there; I wished I hadn't come. My stomach felt empty. I turned around quickly to leave.

"May." I had my back to him. "Is something wrong?"

I hated that question. It made me think I could break. I held my breath and looked up; then I turned around to face him. He looked worried. I think it was the first time that I had seen a man look worried, worried about me.

I'd seen that look on my father's face one morning when he came to pick me up and take me out for the day. He had parked his car outside. It was a silver Cadillac, and there was a small new dent in the side. He ran his hand up and down it, and said, "I can't fucking believe it." We were going to the park, but we had to go to the garage first. We passed a stereo shop on the way. It was closed, but my father looked in the window for a while.

"Come here," Rufus said. I followed him into his room. There were piles of books, papers, and a typewriter on his desk. There was a piece of paper in the typewriter.

The bed was messy, unmade. I sat on it. He sat down in the wooden chair at the desk.

"What are you writing?" I asked, looking at the typewriter.

"I'm trying to figure out a word."

"A word?"

"I've been trying to figure it out for days. There's really no word like it in English."

"Maybe you should make one up then," I said.

He smiled at me. "That's a really good idea."

I wrapped my hands around my toes. I was happy now that he thought I had a good idea. It made me feel more comfortable, sitting on his bed in the middle of the night, for no reason at all.

"Are you cold?" he asked, as he walked over to the dresser. He pulled out a pair of socks and a green sweater.

"I like this sweater, it's soft." I put it on, and the socks, but I was still shivering. Once I get cold I stay cold for a long time.

"Let's make some tea," he said, standing up. We walked up the narrow back stairs to the guests' kitchen. The cupboard was full of teas, biscuits, and cereals. There was milk in the fridge, and butter, and room for whatever the guests wanted to keep in it. In the summer it is full of brown paper bags with names written on them. Sometimes Jolene and I would sneak our hands in and feel around. We'd break pieces off Toblerone bars and take handfuls of wild strawberries, then eat them really quickly.

Rufus turned the light on. It was a dim yellow. Even though no one could hear us, we whispered when we spoke. He filled the kettle and put it on the stove.

"Eden and I painted the cupboards white last summer for two pounds each. We got into a fight, and he threw his paintbrush at my face."

"What did you fight about?" he asked, taking two cups out. He was trying not to smile.

"He was too slow, and I told him he was stupid." Rufus thought that was funny, I could tell.

"Are there any biscuits? We'll have a midnight snack. This is like boarding school," he said. "Don't tell your mother I let you stay up so late."

"I don't care, I hate school. I hate Madame Monet; she's my French teacher."

"I didn't like French either." He opened a packet of chocolate cream biscuits. I took one.

"Is Patricia your girlfriend?" It just came out. That happened to me when I felt safe with someone, I would say anything.

It stopped him for a moment. Everything got slow; his hand rested on top of the cereal box. I hoped he wouldn't suddenly turn into a serious man. I didn't like them, they said things to me like: "Now that was a stupid question, wasn't it?" or "Curiosity killed the cat." He might say, "It's really none of your business." I stood still for a moment, waiting.

"She's not my girlfriend," he said. "She worked at my publisher's, and that's how we met and dated a bit. You can have many different types of relationships in your life. We had fun together, but I don't think either of us took this one very seriously."

I thought about her voice on the phone and how it was like an arrow. I wanted to tell him that she had asked if my mother was committing adultery, but it embarrassed me to say it. A week had gone by since that night, and she hadn't phoned again. That conversation seemed like it might not really have happened. I was thinking of Patricia at the office.

"She's pretty." I don't know why I said it. I think I was trying to compliment him.

We made mint tea with milk. It was warm in the kitchen. We sat across from each other at the square table next to the window.

"Do you like living here?" he asked me.

"Sometimes," I said, but I wasn't really sure. I liked it now. This was fun, sitting at the table drinking tea, eating chocolate biscuits. Outside the window everything was black—there was no moon that night; it had disappeared like my mother—but if you looked up you could see the stars and know there was still a sky.

...

At school the next day Barbara Whitmore had a stack of pink sealed envelopes in her hand. They were birthday party invitations, I could tell. I looked away, pretending I didn't care.

Once, I overheard two women talking; they were part of the ladies' group in town that made marmalade and knitted babies' bonnets. They sold them every other Sunday in the church cellar.

One of the women was Emma's mother, a girl in my form. I thought the other one was a bad witch; she had a mole and a squinty eye. Next to them sat Barbara Whitmore's mother. She had a long thin back and ash-blond hair that curled neatly under. She was reading a paperback book, not talking to them, but she could hear what they were saying and she was listening; I could tell.

I was standing at the table behind them, looking at tiny porcelain animals that cost £1.75 each. There were lambs, horses and skunks, and they were small and shiny. I touched each one carefully, trying to decide. Then I heard Emma's mother say "The single woman from London." I froze with my finger on the porcelain spaniel.

"The one what come up from London and bought the old schoolhouse? That one?" That was the woman I thought was a witch. She had a thick voice. I thought she wanted to put a spell on me, and suddenly I felt a pain in my ribs.

Mrs Whitmore looked up from her book and over at them.

"Well, Emma's new coloured pencils went missing right from her cubby." That was Emma's mother, I recognized her prickly voice. I didn't take the pencils.

"Oh," said the witch. "I've seen the girl, a haunting little thing she is."

I waited for more, I would listen to anything, I never closed my eyes at the films, I never covered my ears.

"The corgy's sweet too, the Queen's favourite dog," said the woman selling the miniature animals. She smiled at me, and the room filled up with chatter again. I put my hand in my pocket and handed her a pound; it was all I had plus some change. I wanted the spaniel. I counted the change slowly, waiting to hear if the women behind me would start talking again, but someone else was asking them the price of jam.

I handed her the rest of the money and she put the spaniel in a small brown paper bag. I said, "Thank you," but my voice sounded as though it were coming from somewhere else. I wanted to find a mirror. The two women were still talking to the man who had asked about the jam. He wanted to know how much sugar was in it, because the dentist had told him his teeth were falling out.

"That's a shame," Emma's mother said, sounding sorry. They would talk about him next, so I moved on. There was a small toilet in the back with a mirror in it. I walked towards it with my head down so no one would see me. There was a queue. I stood behind a woman and her son who was holding himself.

When my turn came I turned the latch. There was a small square mirror with rust spots on it, so high up I couldn't see my mouth. I was scared to stare too long. I ran the water and washed my hands with the bar of soap on the sink. I thought I should cut a fringe. There was a knock on the door so I dried my hands on my shirt and left. The queue had grown longer, more parents and children standing cross-legged. It was the beginning of spring and everyone was out.

Outside was bright, the sky blue and clear above, but I had rocks in me. I could only look at the ground. My hair fell over my face. I tied my cardigan around my waist and walked home. That word "haunting" was everywhere: in the cracks of the road, in my maroon sandals, in my hands; it was in the little brown paper bag with the porcelain spaniel that I held tightly.

This is how things happen on a spring day: a young bird sitting on the grass gets caught by a dog, a car drives too fast into another one, someone says one word that you hear. Just one word. Birds bleed too. The clocks are all wrong.

At home, in front of the full-length mirror in my mother's bathroom, I took the scissors out and cut a fringe. Then I realized it was my clothes, the colour of my clothes. I needed bright colours and some pastels.

When my mother came in, I said, "I don't want to live here any more." I thought it was the house; the dead schoolgirls who disappeared in the rocks had come back to haunt the house, and now I was haunted too. It was the house's fault.

My mother put her arms around me, and my shoulders started to shake and then I was crying. It was loud in the bathroom. "What happened? What happened?" she kept asking, holding me close. There was a wet patch on her shoulder. I didn't answer, I couldn't. I didn't want anyone else to know what that woman had said about me, not even my mother. Especially not my mother.

She took me into the kitchen and gave me a glass of Ribena. I was thirsty, my face was hot. She watched me drink; then she said, "If you don't tell me what's wrong, I can't help you."

"I need new clothes," I told her. I thought she would say I had enough, but we got into the car and went to the big children's clothes store. It took twenty minutes to get there. They only sold new clothes, there was no second-hand rack in the back. She bought me a pink button-down shirt, and ankle socks with ruffled cuffs, and fuzzy hair clips with fish on them. Eden didn't get anything. I could tell she thought they were ugly—"hideous" is the word she would have used. The clothes she chose for me were from other countries, India and Romania, but she pretended she liked the new ones. "Is this what everyone's wearing here?" she asked, and I nodded. She didn't complain about how much they cost. Not ever, not even when the bills came that month.

Still, nothing changed, not even when I wore all of them at the same time. Courtney, one of Barbara's friends, asked what were on my clips. "Are those fishies?"

That day, Jolene and I pretended we didn't notice when Barbara handed out her party invitations in class.

...

I was in our sitting room reading for my English class, ten pages a night, when the phone rang. I picked it up and heard my mother say hello.

"Darling!" It was Annabel. "I'm back in London. How are you? Guess who I had lunch with?"

"Who?"

"Patricia. The writer's girlfriend."

"Oh. I don't think she's his girlfriend, Annabel." My mother sounded annoyed.

I covered the mouthpiece with my hand and sat on the floor by the phone. "Anyway." Annabel took a deep exaggerated breath. "How are you? And the children? Is it cold there?"

"Fine. . . . It's not too bad yet. It's very quiet. No one else is here. I haven't had to do much work."

"How's he?"

"Eden?"

"No, him." Then, in a whisper, "The old fusspot writer."

"Rufus? Fine, fine. He turned out to be very nice. . . . He's not a fusspot at all, actually. We've become quite good friends."

Every time I heard her say "friends" I relaxed. Friends are just friends: they don't kiss, they don't have sex, they don't commit adultery. Friends: a safe thing to be.

"You have?" I heard Annabel light a cigarette.

"It's nice for me to have someone to talk to here besides the children and the ceiling." It was true; all her friends lived in London.

"I'm the first one to tell you to come back to London during the winter." Annabel was full of good ideas. "All right, darling, I'll let you go, I just wanted to—"

"What did she say?" my mother asked in one breath.

"What? Oh, Patricia."

"Mmm." That was my mother trying to sound like she could take it or leave it.

"Well, she works at his publishing company. Did you know that? Apparently she's very clever. That's how they met and started dating."

"According to him they had a casual fling and that was it. He never talks about her." That was my mother talking quickly, a typewriter.

"You know how men are, they don't talk, especially to other women. They like to seem cool. She makes it sound as if he's absolutely mad about her. . . . Anyway, she's very sweet. We had lunch at that little place off the Kings Road, the Italian place. She had one of those bags I saw in American *Vogue*. I have to find one. She thought you were so nice. She was asking all about you. . . . She said she knew someone who would be perfect for you. . . . I told her you were single."

"I'm not interested, and you can tell her. I have to give Eden his bath."

"Darling, did you get up on the wrong side of the bed this morning? Anyway, I've found the curtain fabric for your sitting room."

"Oh. What colour is it?" my mother asked.

"A beautiful lavender colour. My lady in Edgware is making them. Patricia and I were talking about coming up sometime next week."

"Patricia's coming? Rufus hasn't said anything." She sounded like she was biting something.

"Lucy, calm down to a panic."

"No, it's just that I would like to know for sure because I have to fix up a room. You know."

I put the phone down slowly. Patricia was coming. I ran my finger over the table; it was dusty. Patricia was coming. We'd have to clean.

Eleven

I never gave the note to my mother. The one from my French teacher, Madame Monet. She was supposed to sign it, and I was supposed to give it back to Madame Monet. But I didn't. It was still in my satchel with a packet of half-eaten crisps. I always sat in the back, looking down at the top of my desk, hoping she wouldn't see me.

Madame Monet hadn't asked for the note, I thought she had forgotten. There was a black-and-white clock on the classroom wall, and the second hand ticked and ticked. One day, as I was pushing books into my bag and walking towards the door, I heard her call my name. I ignored it and kept walking, until I felt a hand on my shoulder. It was her, Madame Monet. I turned around to get her hand off me.

"I would like to speak with you a moment, May."

"Now?" I asked.

"Yes." She looked at me as though she had just tasted something sour.

"Okay." The other girls turned their heads as they left the classroom.

"Come over to my desk."

I looked at Jolene, who was standing by the door, and rolled my eyes. She was bad at French too, but not as bad as me. That was only because her mother sat her down at the dining-room table and made her do the homework. Then she checked, every page, through the glasses at the end of her nose.

"Wait for me."

"I have to go to the horrible dentist," Jolene said, making a face.

"I'll phone you later." I wanted Madame Monet to know that we were going to talk about her. I walked over to her desk and looked up at the map of France on the wall.

"Do you have the note?" She was a tall, thin woman. Every day she ate an apple and cheese for lunch.

"I forgot to bring it, Mrs Monet." This is how I pronounced her name: Mon-*ate*.

"Madame Monet." She said it very slowly. "Now repeat after me."

"Madame Mo-*net*," I said, following her lips.

"Monet! It is a silent *t. Encore!*" She held one finger out like a conductor's stick.

"Madame Monet."

"*Bien!*" She was smiling, waving her finger in the air. She liked the sound of her own name. "See, that was much better. You just need to try harder. This will be where you sit from now on." She pointed to the middle desk in the front row.

"Okay," I said, but she stood in front of me shaking her head.

"What do you say?" she asked, holding her lips tightly together.

"*Oui,* Madame Monet."

She clapped her hands together, then patted me on the forehead. "If you start doing your lessons, I won't ask you to give the note to your mother."

"Okay." I bent down to pick my satchel up from the floor. I wanted to say thank you but I felt shy. It's hard to be nice. But then I said it. "Thank you. I will try to do my lessons every night. I promise." I meant it. I really wanted to.

"It's not that hard. You're a smart girl."

That made me want to cry. This is what happens when people are nice: It makes me want to cry.

...

The schoolyard was empty. Everyone had been picked up, everyone had gone home. It was past four. The sky was grey and looked like it might storm. I was going home, straight to my room, to do my French homework. That was the first thing I would do every day after school.

As I walked towards the gates I saw a group of girls on the bench, gathered around someone, someone taller than them. An older girl, someone's older sister, a girl from the college. I would have to pass them, but the path was wide. I put my head down, pretending to kick something, a pebble. I was scared of groups of girls. I thought they were always talking about me. If I heard them laugh, I thought it was me they were laughing at.

"May! May! Come here." One of the girls was standing up, waving at me. I took a few steps forward and so did the girl. It was Barbara Whitmore. She had never shouted my name or waved to me before, so I wasn't sure what she wanted. I walked towards her and smiled, acting like this was normal. I buttoned my coat. She had never been mean, she just ignored me. When we were younger and it was important to be good at games, she never picked me to be on her team. I would stand in the middle of the gym with Jolene and the three other girls like us, waiting, pretending not to care, hoping I was the next one chosen so I wouldn't be left standing in the middle of the gym.

Barbara's two best friends, Courtney and Polly, were sitting on the bench next to a tall girl with short blond hair. I always overheard them talking about clubs and boys and cigarettes and being drunk. I thought, When do they do their French lessons? They looked at me, but it was a different kind of look. As I walked closer, the tall girl in the middle stood up. It was Patricia.

"May, sweetie, give me a hug!" She rushed towards me and wrapped her arms around me. Everyone watched. I thought, What is she doing here?

"I came to pick you up from school," she said loudly. "Why were you so late? I thought I'd missed you, but these girls told me you were still here."

"I had to talk to a teacher." I took a small step back. I thought I would fall.

"Did you get into trouble?" Polly asked.

"You know Jet Jones!" Barbara said, pushing Polly out of the way. Jet Jones was the man who sang that song that was always on the radio. I didn't know him, but I had seen him on *Top of the Pops*. All the girls were looking at me. I hadn't said anything yet. I didn't know what they were talking about.

"Jet loves May!" Patricia told them. "He always said if she was just a little older she would be the perfect girl for him!"

"He did?" They all turned to look at me again, studying me, trying to figure it out. Patricia nodded, smiling.

"Did he ever touch you?" That was Courtney. She was the first girl in our form to French-kiss a boy. "Did he? Or did he ever kiss you on the cheek or something?"

I stood there, I didn't know what to say. I kept thinking that this must be a joke they were playing on me. It was a trick. I thought I should walk away.

"What do you think of my new do? You haven't even mentioned it," Patricia said, holding her hands out around her head. She had cut her hair short, just below her ears, a bob; everyone was getting them. She walked over to me and put her arm around my shoulders.

"It looks nice," I said.

"It's very French," Polly told her. She was sitting on the bench smoking a cigarette.

"What kind of shampoo do you use?" Barbara asked. "It's so shiny." The girls lifted their faces up to look at her. I looked too. She looked older with her hair short.

"Vidal Sassoon," she told them, and they nodded, slowly, the way you do when something's really interesting. We were quiet for a moment staring at Patricia. She was wearing a little baby-blue shirt and black pedal-pusher trousers, black flat shoes. Her stomach was flat. She had a thin, short, beige rain jacket on top and a matching baby-blue suede handbag with a fringe. I think it was the one Annabel said she saw in American *Vogue*.

"So tell us. Did he?" Suddenly Courtney was staring right at me. I nodded slowly, imagining him kissing me.

"I would have died! I can't believe it, I would have died!" Courtney and Barbara had their hands over their mouths, screaming; their faces turned red. But Polly just sat on the bench, one leg crossed over the other, swinging the top one back and forth, like a bell.

"Where? Which cheek?" they wanted to know.

"He's kissed her lots of times," Patricia told them.

"Did it make you feel all tingly?" Courtney asked, in a whisper. "I get shivers just thinking about him."

"No. He's like an older brother," I said. It was easy, making things up. It becomes real; it was real at that moment.

"Like an older brother?" They all stopped with their mouths open. "You're good friends with him?"

I was getting nervous. What if they wanted to meet him or see pictures? "But he's been really busy lately with his singing."

"He flew to Italy last night," Patricia said.

"Oh," they said, sounding disappointed. As if they'd been told to read a book over the Christmas holidays.

"I have lots of homework to do," I said. I wanted to go home, to see someone I knew, my mother.

"I parked my car down the street," Patricia said.

"'Bye, May. 'Bye, Patricia. See you tomorrow, May." I wasn't used to them talking to me, so I just waved and walked away.

I wondered what the girls would do when we left. I thought they might go to an older boy's house, sit on the rug in his bedroom listening to records, smoking cigarettes. Barbara and Courtney would sing along, Polly would tap her foot.

Patricia and I walked to her car. The sky was darker now. The shopkeepers were closing up, turning the signs around, pulling down blinds, sweeping floors.

When I was sure we were far enough away, I said, "Why did you tell them I know Jet Jones?" I tried to sound obnoxious like I thought she was stupid, the way the kids in American movies speak.

"It's true, he really is my brother," she said, turning to me.

"But I don't know him and they'll find out." I was afraid they would tell everyone in school, and Jolene would hear and know it was a lie.

"They'll never know unless you tell them. You'll meet him one day." I didn't believe he was her brother. I thought she would have told me before.

She stopped in front of a navy blue car. It looked new. I didn't want to get in the car with her.

"I'll walk home," I said, and turned to leave.

She grabbed me by the arm. "Don't be silly, May."

"How did you start talking to them?" I asked her. I was curious because I had never been able to.

"I was waiting for you so I asked one of them if they knew you and we started talking. . . . I was trying to make them like you, May," she said, opening the car door.

We sat in the car and closed the doors. Patricia turned the key and the radio came on too loud. It made us jump in our seats. I tried not to ask, but I had to know. "How did you know they didn't like me? I mean, what did they say?"

She looked at me and sighed. We were driving down the road, "Are you hungry?" she asked, looking at the stores on the street.

"What did they say?" I needed to know; I wanted to know what was wrong with me.

"They didn't *say* anything." She stressed the word "say". "I could tell . . . There was a group of them at my school too. It's always the same, nothing ever changes. Where's the shop that sells those vegetable pastries?"

"Down that road." I pointed to the left. "It's quite far, at the end." We didn't speak for a moment. Then I said, "But you were probably part of that group."

"Eventually I was," she said, looking straight ahead.

. . .

When we got home, I went right upstairs and locked the door to our flat. It was an old lock we never used; we never needed to. My mother and Rufus were in the kitchen, sitting at the table over the Scrabble board. The radio was on and they were singing.

"Who's winning?" I asked, walking in.

"He won the first game but I won the second, and now he's exactly ten points behind me."

"We've been playing since two," Rufus said. He looked happy, sitting up straight, smiling. There was a bottle of wine on the table and a box of biscuits, plain ones covered in milk chocolate. They had a picture of a boy holding a flute on them. They were from Germany.

"Can I have one?" I don't know why I asked. I usually just take things right off her plate.

"Of course you can. I bought them specially for you." They were my favourites. I was glad to see Rufus. I wanted him to help with my homework.

"Can you help me with my French tonight? It's important."

"What are you doing?" he asked.

"I'm not sure, I'm behind."

"Are you hungry? I was going to make beans on toast," my mother asked us.

"Beans on toast. I've never had that before," Rufus said. He thought he was funny, and she did too. I sat down with them and ate the chocolate from around the edges of the biscuit. It was nice to be with them in the kitchen with the wine and Scrabble and the door locked.

"I'll help you," Rufus told me.

My mother was looking at her letters, picking them up, moving them around, putting them back down. I looked over at them, but I couldn't see any words. It's annoying having someone look over your shoulder, so I stopped. When I looked up, Rufus was staring at us.

"Just then you two looked exactly alike. I never thought that before." This made my face feel hot. My mother was pretty, not in the same way Patricia was but the way a shell is, or a leaf, something you have to pick up and hold up to the light and turn around and around in your hand to see clearly.

"I like Patricia's new haircut." I said it quickly, I didn't want him to talk about how I looked any more.

"What?"

My mother looked up at him, holding a square wooden letter between her fingers.

"Patricia's new haircut?" he went on, as though he didn't understand what I was saying.

I nodded. "It's short." I moved my hands to my ears, trying to explain to him.

"Patricia's not here," he said.

"I saw her after school in town." He looked confused, and my mother was still holding the letter.

"You saw Patricia in town?"

I nodded again.

"It was probably just someone who looked like her, but with short hair. She wouldn't cut her hair." He said this to my mother. She looked back down at the Scrabble board.

"No, I talked to her. She drove me home."

"She's here? Right now?" he asked. He looked worried.

"Yes. I mean, I think so." I came right upstairs but I remembered hearing her car door close.

"Did she tell you she was coming?" he asked my mother. There was an advertisement on the radio. She stood up and turned it off. "Lucy." He said her name softly, as though he were bending down to pick up something that might break.

"What?" She was standing near the counter with her hand on the radio.

"Did she tell you she was coming?"

"No, she didn't." That's what it is like here: empty rooms; anyone can come. We need the money. "I have to put sheets on the bed. Or is she going to sleep in your room?"

You couldn't see anything on my mother's face, but her voice sounded as if she were talking to a stranger. To a guest. He just sat there looking at her. She went to the fridge and opened it.

"No, she's not going to sleep in my bed." He sounded angry.

"Maybe I should make cauliflower and cheese instead. Does that sound good, May? Eden likes it." She closed the fridge door and looked around the room at the walls, like she was looking for a clock. "What time is it?"

"I think it's around six or something," I said.

"Six? I have to collect Eden." Eden was at his little friend Jake's house. They spent hours building forts for their Action Men. He liked it better at Jake's house because I wasn't there. Once, they had left the men set up in fighting positions, and Jolene and I came in and stole their clothes and put them in our Cindy doll's ballerina outfits. There was no one to bother them at Jake's house.

"Do you want me to come with you?" he asked. She went to the sink and turned the tap on.

"You should go down and see Patricia," she said, rinsing her hands.

"Aren't you going to help me with my French?" I asked him.

"I can help," my mother said, but I didn't want her to. She wasn't good at French either.

Rufus stood up. I thought we would go to my room and he would give me all the answers, but then the phone rang. The three of us stood, looking at it. No one moved. It rang again and again. Finally my mother picked it up.

We stood by the door waiting; she had her back turned to us.

"How are you? . . . I'm well, thank you. . . . May's right here." She held the phone out to me.

It was Jolene. She wanted to know what Madame Monet had said to me. "Did you get in trouble?" she asked, as though it were a happy question.

"I'm going to pick up Eden," my mother said, and walked out of the kitchen. Rufus stood there for a moment; then he followed. I heard him call her name.

"No, she was nice," I told Jolene.

"She was?"

"Yup."

"Really?" She sounded disappointed.

I could hear them talking at the end of the hall by the stairs. I untwisted the phone cord and stretched it to the doorway, but I couldn't hear what they were saying.

"What did she want to talk to you about?" she asked again.

I remembered that Barbara, Courtney and Polly all thought I knew Jet Jones. I walked back inside the kitchen, holding on to the phone cord.

"Did I ever tell you that I know Jet Jones?" I said.

"No, because you don't."

"I do."

"No, you don't, May."

"Yes, I do, Jolene."

"If you do, why haven't you ever told me before? When did you meet him?"

"In London. He's my friend's brother." I couldn't tell her the friend was Patricia, because she knew I had just met her.

"You're mad," Jolene said, laughing.

"I have to do my French lessons. The writer man said he would help me. He knows lots of languages." I was getting worried that Rufus would go downstairs and never come up again.

"All right then, see you tomorrow." She sounded upset. I had never got off the phone to do homework before.

I walked down the hallway to the stairs where I'd heard Rufus call my mother's name, but they weren't there. I looked in the sitting room, then my mother's bedroom, but they were both empty.

I went to my room and took the French book out of my satchel. I put it carefully on my desk. I took off my shoes by stepping on the heel, something my mother always said not to do. I sat down at my desk and opened the book, a big hardback that explained all the grammar. We were on page fifty. I read it but didn't understand. I reread it but nothing stayed with me. The *cahier* in which we have to translate sentences, put things in the past tense, and use pronouns looked dead in front of me. I had hardly written anything in it all year and didn't know how to start; I was too far behind. I smashed the pencil point into the open book. It's hard to change yourself.

...

Later, I heard the sound of running water and Eden's voice. I walked towards the bathroom door; he was telling Mum about what he had done at Jake's house. His voice was bright, like Christmas lights.

I opened the door and walked in. Eden was sitting on the toilet with his knickers hanging down around his ankles. His feet didn't even touch the floor. I thought he might fall into the toilet. He stopped talking when he saw me; then it was just the sound of the running water. My mother sat on the edge of the tub, with her sleeves rolled up. She ran her hand through the water, stirring it, like a pot of porridge. She had done this for me when I was little, mixing the water, making sure it wasn't too hot or too cold in any one place.

"I can't do a poo," Eden said. He pushed himself up off the toilet and pulled his knickers up.

I sat down on the edge of the tub. The air was warm and steamy.

"Did he come up and help you with your French?" she asked me, dragging her hand through the water. She knew he hadn't. She hadn't been gone very long.

"Who?" I said, pretending that I didn't care about him, that I had already forgotten.

"Rufus."

"No."

She turned off the taps. "I'll help you, after I give Eden his bath."

"I don't need help." I'd filled in the blanks in the workbook. They were probably wrong, but it would look like I had done something when I sat in the middle desk in the front row tomorrow.

She put a green dinosaur sponge in the tub. It floated around all alone.

"Does she look pretty with short hair?"

What she really meant was, Is he in love with her?

I nodded and said, "She's really pretty."

"Mum. Mum, I think you're pretty," Eden said, stepping into the tub. She smiled at him, the way someone smiles who is half asleep, and it disappears before it's even a full smile. He stood naked, with one hand on her shoulder and just his feet in the water.

"I can't believe she arrived without telling him. I would never do that." That was the difference between her and Patricia. Some people risk everything. They'll get dressed up, wait on the doorstep with open arms. "Take me, I'm yours. You can have me entirely," they say. Other people just turn around, quietly folding their wings across their chest.

I took off my socks and put my feet in the water.

"Take them out!" Eden yelled at me.

"Don't be silly, she can put her feet in the water," my mother told him.

He sat down slowly in the warm bathwater. You could see thin blue veins under his eyes and in his hands and feet. He looked young and new; his heart was still close to his mouth. He said things like "Mum, I think you're pretty." He could stand naked in front of her, with his feet in the water and his hand on her shoulder.

My mother took the white bar of soap and rubbed it into the dinosaur. She moved the sponge in circles around his shoulders and back and neck, then gently behind his little ears.

There was the sound of car doors closing outside. My mother stood up with the sponge in her hand and walked over to the small window above the sink.

"I wonder where they're going," she said to the window. The sponge dripped down the side of her jeans and onto the floor.

We heard the motor start and the sound a car makes when it drives away. Eden sat still in the bath, with the soapsuds on his back and neck, looking at her.

"They're probably going out for a romantic dinner," I said, throwing it at her back.

When she walked over to the bath, she moved slowly, as though she were walking through water. She knelt down next to the tub and squeezed the sponge out. Her arm hung in the water, holding the sponge. She was still; Eden was still. I wiggled my feet and splashed him.

"Did you make cauliflower and cheese?" I asked.

"No." She didn't look at me. "We bought fish and chips on the way home. They're in the kitchen."

I pulled my feet out of the water and stood on the bath mat. I was hungry.

"Why do you think that?" my mother asked, as she squeezed the water from the sponge down Eden's back, rinsing him.

"What?"

"That they're going out for a romantic dinner? They're probably talking about his work." Sometimes it was like this with us: darts.

"Why do you care anyway?" I asked, standing at the door. Eden hadn't moved; he sat straight up in the tub. The water didn't even move.

"I don't care," she said. Everything that was curious, everything that was like a girl, like a butterfly in her, fell out. "I wasn't even talking to you," she said. "I was just talking to myself."

Then I left and closed the door behind me, and all I could hear was the light sound of the water swaying in the tub.

Twelve

I stood outside the girls' lavatory waiting for Jolene. The lunch bell had just rung and all the girls walked by in twos and threes, shoulder to shoulder, on their way to the dining hall. I was standing there with nothing to do, so I bent down to pull up my socks. Someone shouted my name. "May!"

When I looked up, Barbara was standing in front of me, smiling.

"Hi." I was looking at her frock. It came to the middle of her thigh; mine fell past my knee.

"Come here," she said, waving her hand for me to follow. We walked down the hall to the cubbyholes. She stopped in front of hers and took out her red heart-shaped handbag.

"Here." She held out a pink envelope. "It's an overnight."

My name was written on it in big squiggly letters—*May*—and it was underlined.

"Thanks." I held it in my hand like a medal.

"It's going to be so much fun," Barbara said, hugging her heart-shaped bag to her stomach.

I nodded, smiling. She made me nervous because I thought I would have to be fun.

"We're going to stay up all night!" she said. I looked down the hall to see if Jolene was coming, but she wasn't. She took a long time in the loo.

"What do you want for a present?" I asked.

"I don't know." She took a lipstick out of the bag. It smelled like pink gum.

"Barbara, come on!" Courtney shouted from the other end of the hallway. I imagined myself standing with them, the four of us.

"Polly wants a fag," Barbara said. They hardly ate lunch, they just hung out in the school yard and smoked cigarettes. She ran down the hall, her skirt flying up behind her; I could see the tops of her legs and her white knickers. Suddenly, she stopped and ran back towards me.

"I know! I know what I want," she said, catching her breath. "I want a photo of Jet." Then she spun around and ran down the hallway to where Courtney and Polly stood waiting with their hands on their hips.

I stood there, clutching the envelope in my hand. She wanted a picture of Jet.

The bathroom door opened and Jolene walked out; two other girls came out after her, holding their noses and waving their hands in front of their faces. I went over to my cubby and hid the invitation between the pages of my maths book. I wouldn't tell Jolene.

...

Every puddle was a danger. I kept thinking, What if I trip and fall? All my books would fly through the air like in a cartoon and the invitation would land in a puddle, the pink envelope sinking in the mud. Then I worried I might lose it, leave it somewhere on the bus. So I held the bag tightly, on my lap, like a baby.

Finally I had brought something back from school that I could shout about. It wasn't a report card; it wasn't a blue ribbon or a part in the school play. I had something better than that.

"Mum! Mum!" I said it like a song as I walked into the kitchen. She was on the phone. She put her finger up to her lips, telling me to be quiet. She had a pen in her hand; she was writing things down as she spoke. "Yes. . . . Okay, I will." It was probably the bank. She would hang up the phone and say, "We're broke."

I sat down at the table and waited. I felt happy in a way I never had before, excited. The way my mother and her friends would get in London before they went out to a party or on a date. I stood up and practised doing pliés. I wanted to get skinny before the party. When she put the phone down I said, "Look!" I waved the invitation in my hand like a flag.

"What?" She looked serious.

"I've been invited to Barbara Whitmore's birthday party!"

I thought she would lift me up, hug me, swing me around. But she didn't say anything. She just stood there in an old brown skirt and a big sweater that had so many different colours it looked like a sewing cloth.

"Isn't she the one who's mean to you?"

"Mean to me" stuck to my chest.

"No." I stared back at her like she was stupid, but she was my mother and knew things about me. The first time we had swimming lessons at school I had worn a bikini. My grandmother had sent it to me from Rhode Island; it had red, yellow, and green squares on it and a tie string at the back. All the other girls wore the school swimming costume: a navy blue one-piece. My mother hadn't bought me one. "They won't care about a silly swimming costume. It's a waste of money," she had said, when we were in the uniform shop.

The teacher was standing at the other end of the pool talking to the lifeguard. Barbara swam up behind me and pulled the string undone, then Courtney grabbed the front and pulled it away through the water. I wrapped my arms around my chest. My body felt hot. The pool was a soft blue and I wanted to hide under the water. I started crying and my tears felt like blood; I thought they would turn the water red. They were laughing and pointing and calling each other's names. "Catch the bikini top! Catch the bikini!" they shouted to each other.

Then a girl dropped a towel in the water for me. It was the podgy girl in our class, Jolene. I wrapped the wet towel around me. I could barely stand on the wet tiles; my body felt shaky. Jolene put her hand on my back and walked me to the changing room. I thought, I will never wear a bikini again, never.

"That was a long time ago!" I yelled this at my mother. I was new then. Things like that didn't happen any more.

"Sorry," she said. "I didn't know you had become friends with her."

"Well, I have. See?" I held out the invitation, but she didn't touch it. "Only seven girls were invited. Jolene wasn't invited, only the popular girls."

I thought, She's my mother, she should cheer for me.

"Why wasn't Jolene invited?"

"Because they're not friends. Anyway, Jolene doesn't like her." Jolene was scared of her.

My mother just stared at me.

"You should be happy for me that I was invited; it's important." My French homework, Barbara's party, my father: three important things.

"Of course I'm happy, if you're happy." But she kept looking at me like something smelled bad.

...

I went to my room and opened the envelope with a knife, carefully, so it wouldn't tear. Inside was a white card with tiny pink baby roses around the edges. In the middle of the green leaves and roses it read, *You are invited to a birthday party! 18th of December at 6 p.m. 7 Lamppost Lane. A tea party and overnight.* On the top it said, *To May, from Barbara.* To May, from Barbara. I read that part over and over: To May, from Barbara.

I put it on my chest of drawers and leaned it up against the mirror, right in the middle.

I wanted to tell someone. Someone who would say, "Congratulations!" Like it was an award, which it was.

...

"Patricia!" I called her name as I walked down the hall. I already felt new again, excited.

A door opened slowly, the one across from Rufus's room. Patricia stood there, in a white T-shirt and grey sweatpants, something my mother would have worn. I wondered if she was sick.

"May." She said my name softly, slowly, like a sad word.

"Guess what?"

"What?" Her eyes looked puffy.

"Barbara invited me to her birthday party!"

"She did? That's great." Her voice rose a little to meet mine.

"It's an overnight. Only seven girls were invited."

"That's really great, May." She smiled at me. "I knew they would like you. They just needed to know there was something special about you."

"Something special" lit a fire inside me.

"Come in and talk to me." She looked as though something had been taken out of her.

I stepped into the room. The curtains were closed; there was an open suitcase on the bed.

She said, "Shut the door."

I did, and when I came back she was sitting on the edge of the bed staring at the wall. I sat down on the bed too. She leaned over and ran her fingers through my hair.

"I wish I could be here. I would blow-dry your hair straight and put my special cream in it that makes it smooth. I could make you look pretty." Her voice sounded faded.

I thought maybe someone had died.

"Barbara wants a photo of Jet." I thought she would think that was funny.

She looked up and smiled at me. "She wants a photo? That is so sweet. I have some with me. I wish I was your age. Everything's just starting for you, and everything's ending for me."

She's dying, I thought. She's dying.

She stood up and walked over to the chair that her clothes were piled on. She picked up the baby-blue shirt she had worn yesterday, folded it, and dropped it in the suitcase. I sat on the bed, watching her walk back and forth, picking up clothes, folding them, dropping them in the suitcase. She hardly picked up her feet when she walked, like an old person.

Then she fell into the chair, right on top of her clothes, and put her face in her hands. Her shoulders began to shake. She made loud crying sounds, like a baby. I thought she was pretending, but when she looked up her cheeks were wet and her eyes were red.

"He wants me to leave," she said.

"What?" The words were so quiet I hardly heard them.

"Rufus wants me to leave. He said it was better if he was here working alone."

That was a lie, I thought. Working, he never worked. He was always in the kitchen with my mother.

"He's at the library today. I mean, I could do that for him." She took a deep breath and then she said, "I think they're having an affair. He didn't want me to sleep in his bed; he wouldn't even try to kiss me." Her voice cracked and then she started again, with her head in her hands and her shoulders shaking.

I thought I should walk over to her and put my hand on her back, the way my mother does with me and Eden, but I just sat there on the edge of the bed watching her cry. Suddenly she stopped and looked up at me.

"Are they?"

"They're just friends," I said. It was true; I'd checked. They slept in different beds, and I had heard her say it to Suzy on the phone. "We're just friends," she said. She would have told Suzy. And I would have seen it. In London she always kissed Paul in front of me. They would lie down on the sofa together. I could hear them breathing and moving around behind me while I watched the telly. Then my mother would say, "We're going to take a little nap," and the two of them would go into her bedroom and close the door.

"What do they do together?" Patricia asked.

"What?"

"What do Rufus and Lucy do together?"

I squinted, like I was trying to remember. "They play Scrabble sometimes."

"Scrabble?" Her eyes lifted a little. "That's boring."

I nodded. "And once they went grocery shopping."

"Grocery shopping?" Her voice began to sound like it usually did.

I nodded again. She put her thumbnail in her mouth and stared at the floor. Then she jumped up and walked to the mirror.

"Are you sure my hair looks good this short?" She looked at herself sideways. Then she said, "Well, has he ever taken her out to dinner?"

I was thinking about Patricia blow-drying my hair straight, while I looked through her makeup bag. Two girls in the bathroom getting ready for a party.

"No." I said it like it was the last word in the world.

She walked around the room, back and forth, pacing. Something had woken up in her; she flung her arms down at her sides. "Then why is he being like this?" she asked, looking up at the ceiling, as if it would tell her.

"Maybe he's acting like a cat," I said.

"A cat?" She said it slowly, like she was looking for something in it.

"My mother left me with my grandmother in America when I was little once. And when Mum came back to get me at the railway station, I wouldn't talk to her. I wouldn't even look at her. She said I was like a cat because that's what cats do; they get mad and won't talk to you if you leave them." I didn't remember it happening; my mother told me.

Patricia stood in the middle of the room, nodding.

"You're right," she said. "Maybe he's cross that I left before." Her eyes were wide. "May, you're so smart."

"Do you know how to speak French?" The word "smart" reminded me.

"I understand a little." She looked around the room like it was the first time she had ever seen it. "You're right. I can stay if I want to; it's a hotel." She nodded as if she were agreeing with herself.

I remembered my mother saying, "It's a hotel; we need the money, darling." A room for anyone.

She pulled the curtains open, but no light came in the room. It was already dark out. She turned on the lamp by the bed. She was busy now, opening the bedside drawer, looking for something. I stood up to leave. She took out a thin black leather book, opened it, and ran her finger slowly down the list of names and telephone numbers.

"I have to do my homework now," I said, because I was just standing there.

She looked up, holding her finger in place.

"I'll see you later, May," she said, waving her other hand at me.

...

On my way upstairs I saw Rufus; he was standing by the front door carrying a book. I tried to walk past him.

"Hi, May."

I stopped. He had a brown coat on, it was buttoned up wrong.

"Hi." I started to walk up the stairs.

"Do you want me to help you with your French? I can come now if you want."

"Right now?" I asked. I was serious; I needed to do it.

He nodded.

"Thanks," I said.

He followed me up the stairs. His footsteps sounded heavy behind me. He walked slowly, holding on to the banister.

"I got invited to a party." I couldn't help it. Telling people was the funnest part.

"A party?" he said, behind me.

"My friend Barbara's birthday party." I told him so he would know it wasn't just any party.

"Barbara's birthday party? That will be fun." It was dark on the stairs. You had to walk carefully, looking before you put your foot down.

"When's Lucy's birthday?" He wanted to know when my mother's birthday was.

"The seventh of February."

We walked down the hall to my bedroom. We passed Eden, who was sitting at his desk, swinging his legs underneath like he was listening to a song. "Hi, May! Hi, Rufus!" He waved to us. Sometimes he was like that, excited to see me. "Look, look!" he shouted, running out with a piece of paper in his hand. He held it up in front of us. There were two gold stars on it.

"It had three but one fell off."

"Congratulations!" Rufus said, taking the piece of paper from him. Congratulations. Someone finally said it, but not to me.

"What is it?" I asked.

"My report about trees." Then he stared at Rufus like something was wrong with him. "Why are you wearing a coat?" he asked, squinting up at him.

"I just walked in. I haven't taken it off yet."

"Oh." Eden sounded relieved, like everything was better now he knew.

"Well done, Eden." I said it like a teacher, because I could, because I was his older sister.

Down the hall, I saw my mother pull her bedroom door closed, softly, like a secret.

"Come on," I said to Rufus, and walked to my room.

He sat down in my chair at my desk.

"Aren't you going to take your coat off?"

"I forgot." He unbuttoned his coat and dropped it on the floor next to him. I put the two French books in front of him and sat on my bed.

"What don't you understand?"

"Everything."

"What's that?" He pointed to the window.

"A window." I tried to roll my eyes.

"In French."

"*La fenêtre.*"

"Good."

"What's that?" He pointed to the lamp.

"*La lampe.*" That one was easy. You just had to say it like you were looking at the end of your nose.

"What's that?"

I didn't know. He was pointing to my trainers on the floor, lying toe to toe, like two old rats having a chat. I hoped they didn't smell.

"*Chaussures de tennis*," he said. "You need to make flash cards."

"We have to do the pronouns." I was getting impatient. Today's blank lines in the *cahier* needed to be filled in, like plants that need to be watered. Night was coming. I took my clothes off the chair by the wall and dragged it over to the desk so I could sit next to him. I was hoping he would do the work and I could just watch.

"May, did you bring the post up?" It was my mother. I heard her voice before she walked in the door.

"No." I never bring the post up, I just look through it downstairs to see if there is anything for me. She knew that; she just wanted to come in my room.

"Oh . . . okay." She stood there for a moment, looking at the books on the desk. She was wearing different clothes and her hair was down, brushed smoothly.

When she turned to leave, Rufus said, "Lucy?"

"What?" It was the first time she had looked at him.

"How are you?"

"I'm well, thank you," she said, looking at her hands.

"I went to the library today." He sounded eager, like Eden.

"The one in town? It's the size of a postage stamp."

She was trying to be funny, wanting him to laugh and say, "I know," and they could talk about the man who worked there with the hump on his back, but instead he said, "I like small libraries. I get confused in big ones."

"Oh. Did Patricia go with you?" She hadn't seen him since Patricia arrived, and now she was acting like she hardly knew him.

"No. Patricia's going back to London tomorrow morning."

"Don't you need her to help you?"

"No. I can type."

"She should stay longer. Isn't it nice for her to be out of the city? I haven't even seen her yet." This was my mother pushing Patricia towards him, giving her to him on the palm of her hand, like a small statue.

"I didn't know you wanted to see her." He sounded annoyed.

She opened her mouth but didn't say anything to him. She looked at me and said, "May, are you sure you didn't bring the post up?"

I flipped through the pages of my book, so she would know I was ignoring her.

"All right, I'd better make supper," she said, and then she left.

Rufus watched her walk out. But she didn't go to the kitchen. I heard her walk down the hall into her bedroom and close the door.

He ran his fingers through his hair, then rested his forehead in his hands. He stayed like that, staring down, with his head in his hands. I thought he was thinking about the French, but then he shook his head and said, "Sorry. Let's try to figure this out."

Thirteen

I was late for school the next day. The playground was empty; everyone was inside the classrooms, at their desks. I had heard the bells ringing when I was crossing the main street with the lights. I walked down the hall. All the classroom doors were closed, my footsteps sounded loud beneath me. It was early in the morning and my stomach hurt. This is what school is like for me: the private park in London that only certain people have the key to.

...

In London, there was a park near where we lived with an iron railing around it. The tops pointed up like arrows, so that no one could climb over. Large white houses with long windows stood around it. At night, if the lights were on, you could see inside the rooms; they had deep red walls and heavy curtains. The square-shaped park was just for them.

Our upstairs neighbour in London was an old man, and sometimes I walked his dog for him. The dog's name was Bert; he was a Scottie. He was very old but the man said he was going to live a long time because he always cooked him chicken, rice and vegetables. He made it into a mash; otherwise Bert would just eat the chicken—"Like a naughty boy," the old man would say, shaking his finger, talking in a deep voice, pretending to be angry.

Sometimes I'd walk the dog around the park. Through the fence you could see tulips and rose bushes planted neatly along the path. The stone birdbaths were held by statues of angels. If I were a bird in London, this is where I would live. The trees were so old and tall that when you lifted your head to see the tops, you would see the moon shining through the branches. Inside, a teenage girl with long brown hair held hands with a tall skinny boy as they walked along the gravel path that curved around the grass and the planted flowers. A mother and daughter sat on a bench eating sandwiches.

I walked slowly outside the gate with Bert. Everything seemed so safe, safe in the city, in the park that was separate and clean, and everyone inside had the same key. I thought, They must be rich.

...

I stopped in the school hallway and touched the wall with my fingers. I'd been invited to Barbara's party; things were changing. I opened the classroom door slowly so it wouldn't squeak and stepped inside. The girls turned their heads to look, then back to the teacher. Maths was our first class of the day. Someone from the back of the room stuck up her hand and waved to me. It was Barbara. I waved back, a small wave. Jolene looked behind her to see who I was waving to. When she saw, she looked at me with a tilted expression. I sat down and stared straight ahead at the blackboard.

Fish fingers for lunch, and stewed peaches. Jolene and I sat with our trays at a table near the kitchen.

"Remember, my mum's taking us Christmas shopping tomorrow afternoon," Jolene said.

I nodded. It's hard to talk when you have a secret in your mouth, so I kept it closed.

"I already know what I'm going to give you," Jolene told me. She was trying not to smile. There was a brooch on the collar of her shirt, green-stemmed flowers with little red petals.

"Should we come and pick you up? My mum wants to leave by noon," she said, mixing her peaches and custard together.

"I'll come to your house," I said.

Across the room, Barbara, Courtney, and Polly sat at the corner table picking at their food.

Jolene looked at me. "Aren't you hungry?"

"I have a headache." I didn't really. I saw the three of them huddle together, whispering and then flinging their heads back, laughing.

"You should drink some water," Jolene said. She poured a glass from the jug on the table.

"Thanks." I took a sip. It was warm and cloudy. It always was.

...

I walked up the narrow back stairs to our flat, I didn't want to see anyone and went straight to my room to do my homework. I liked having to do it, sitting before an open book, as though it were a Queen to serve.

I started my maths, to get it out of the way. When I was finished, I remembered it was Friday. The house was quiet. Outside I could hear the wind. The branches of the big tree blew against my window.

I walked down the hallway. "Mum? Eden?" I couldn't speak very loudly. I was scared; it was in my throat. I went into every room, turning on all the lights and then leaving them on. Where was my mother? Where was my brother? I thought, They have disappeared this time, they really have. They went for a walk and they'll never come back, like the schoolgirls who used to live here.

When I turned on the lights in the sitting room, I thought, Something's different in this room; something has changed. I stood in the middle of the room and turned in a slow circle looking at everything: the walls, the ceiling, the floor. The furniture was the same, the ceiling still slanted, the small black-and-white telly was still shoved in the corner. But there was something different. If the room were a woman and you said, "You look pretty. What have you done?" she'd blush slightly, and whisper, "It's my new purple eye shadow." It was something like that in the room.

I stood very still, looking around. The back of my neck felt cold. I thought I could hear voices and music bubbling up through the floor. I bent down, trying to hear the sounds more clearly, but they got lost under the rug. When I looked back up I saw what it was. There were lavender curtains draped around the windows, the curtains Annabel had made in London.

I walked downstairs, stopping on the steps to listen, to make sure. The sounds became louder, clearer, real voices, not like the ones I hear at night that get mixed up in the sea and wind. They were coming from the yellow sitting room downstairs.

The room was warm and looked as though it were lit by candles. A fire burned low in the fireplace. My mother sat in an armchair. A record was playing softly, a French singer, a woman with a high girlish voice. Rufus sat on the sofa holding a wineglass between both hands. Annabel sat across from him, leaning back into her chair, a cigarette in one hand, a glass of wine in the other.

"Do you ever write for magazines?" Annabel asked Rufus. She was still trying to figure out if he was famous.

"I used to," he said, looking down at his glass.

When I walked into the room, my mother's eyes moved over me slowly, looking at me as though she had just left me upstairs in a crib and I had come downstairs almost thirteen years old.

"If it isn't the little cherub," Annabel said when she saw me.

I walked over to give her a kiss on the cheek. "I didn't know you were coming."

"Neither did I," Annabel said, raising her eyebrows, like she was surprised at herself.

"Are you staying for Christmas?" I asked.

"Did you see the curtains?"

I nodded. "They're nice."

"Lady Dorchester has the same ones in her library."

"They're lovely," my mother said.

Eden was sitting next to the fire with a colouring book and a box full of pens and pencils. The cat was next to him. I sat down on the arm of Annabel's chair.

There was a wooden bowl of pistachios on the table and a packet of dates with a thin plastic fork. I took a pistachio and opened the shell.

Patricia walked in. She wore tight dark jeans and a red polo-neck sweater. Everything brand new, the colours still bright. "Sorry I took so long. That shower downstairs is crap," she said, and sat down on the sofa next to Rufus. Their thighs touched and he moved over slightly.

"Have a glass of wine, darling," Annabel said, as she poured a glass.

Annabel had a roughish voice that she tried to make high and elegant whenever she spoke to someone she was trying to impress. It was how she spoke to Patricia.

"Remind me to phone him tomorrow," Patricia said to Annabel.

"I will," Annabel said, handing her the glass of wine. I thought, They must have had more than one lunch together in London.

"Phone who?" my mother asked.

"Didn't I tell you?" Annabel said. My mother shook her head. "Patricia has very kindly recommended that I decorate her brother's house. Jet Jones, the singer."

"He just bought a new house on Primrose Hill," Patricia told my mother.

"It's beautiful," Annabel said.

Patricia looked at my mother. She moved her eyes from the top of my mother's head down to her feet, as though she were trying to figure something out.

"Have you done something to yourself, Lucy? You look different."

The light was dim in the room. There were just two table lamps and the light from the fire. The lamp near my mother had a red shade, and the light from it made her glow.

"No, I don't think so." She put her hand on her neck, something she did when she was nervous. She did look different; there was colour in her face and her hair was down.

Rufus looked over at my mother and smiled. There was an expression on his face that made his eyes light up, the way parents look at their child, proud. Rufus looked at her that way and my mother saw it too. I thought, She knows, she knows. Then why is she sinking into the back of her chair with her hand on her neck?

"It must be the hair. You should wear it down more, it's so nice and thick. Is that a natural wave?" Patricia asked.

My mother nodded.

"You look like that actress with your hair down. What's her name?" Patricia looked to Annabel for help.

I've seen women do this before, act more interested in the woman than the man, making a fuss, telling her she's pretty. Getting her on their side, away from him.

"Oh, I know who you mean!" Annabel said, waving her cigarette in the air. They moved at the same speed, Annabel and Patricia. "That actress. Oh, God, what's her name? You know the one I mean."

Everyone looked at Annabel, waiting for her to figure out who she was talking about.

"I know who you mean," Patricia said, looking at my mother and nodding her head slowly.

"I'm sure Lucy's more beautiful," Rufus said. My mother's face reddened, and she looked down at her hands.

I saw Patricia turn her head very slowly towards Rufus, and when their eyes met she smiled widely at him. "You know just what to say to the women!" she said, laughing, then laid her hand on his knee. My mother looked away. Annabel sipped her wine. No one spoke. The French record played softly in the background, and Patricia moved her hand gently up and down Rufus's leg.

"Lucy?" Patricia said, after a moment. "We were going to go to the films. Would you like to come with us?"

Rufus stood up quickly, and Patricia's hand fell from his knee. He walked over to the record player.

I thought Eden would be bouncing around, wanting to go to the movie, but he just sat there by the cat.

"I don't think I want to go any more," Rufus said.

"Lucy, you probably won't want to go either," Patricia said.

I walked over to the fire to look at Eden's drawing. She'll never go, I thought, she'll never go.

"I'd love to see a film, actually," I heard my mother say. Then she stood up, walked over to where Rufus was standing, and said, "Rufus, come to the films with us."

Eden stood up and followed the cat out of the room. He could do that for hours, follow the cat around.

"Do you want to go?" Rufus asked her quietly, and she nodded her head.

When my mother turned to Patricia, she kept her face very blank as though she were looking at a plain wall and said, "We should leave soon."

...

We stood outside the cinema, waiting in the ticket queue. The wind blew and blew. We wrapped our arms around ourselves and jumped up and down. My hands stung. I'd forgotten my gloves. Where did the winter come from?

My mother made a sound like a gasp and her hand flew up to her mouth. She turned around, looking behind her as though something had just bitten her ankle.

"What?" Annabel asked.

"I don't believe it." She spoke almost in a whisper.

"What?" we all asked, leaning in.

"Where's Eden?" This was louder. Everyone looked frozen for a moment. We turned around, looking behind ourselves.

"Was he in the car?" my mother asked. We went quiet for a moment, thinking. Then we all shook our heads.

"We must have lost him in the shuffle," Annabel said.

Eden, lost in the shuffle. That's what it will say on his tombstone.

"We must have left him at home."

"May, I told you to get him ready."

Then I remembered. My mother had handed me his coat; she was checking in her purse to make sure she had enough money. We were in a rush to get to the cinema on time. I called his name while I walked down the hallway with his coat in my hand, and I found him tiptoeing behind the cat into the bathroom. I came up behind him and grabbed his wrist. "Put this on," I told him. It was brown with wooden buttons, too short in the sleeves and the top button pinched his neck, but I did it up anyway.

"He's following the cat around," I said.

"Why didn't you tell me?" She was asking me because he usually sat next to me in the back.

"It's not her fault," Patricia said.

"I have to go home!" my mother said, flapping her arms around. She started to walk to the car.

"I'll help you look for him," Rufus said, following her.

"Lucy, he's done this before. He probably hasn't even noticed we're gone," Annabel said.

"I was left alone all the time when I was little." I tried to shout it at my mother, but only Annabel and Patricia heard.

"That was in a city, darling; there were neighbours," Annabel told me.

My mother was walking quickly towards the car, arms swinging sharply. Rufus ran up alongside her. I could see their breath in the air.

"Now we'll have to take a bloody taxi home," Annabel said.

"Where's he going?" Patricia asked, as she watched them walk away.

"Next, please," said the woman at the ticket window.

Annabel stepped up to the window. "I don't know how many tickets to buy," she said to the woman in the booth, but the woman just stared at her, bored.

"Four," Patricia said, unzipping a thin brown wallet and handing her a note. Then she put her hand on my shoulder and pulled me out of the queue away from Annabel.

"Go and get him," she said, leaning close to me.

"What?"

"Tell him you want him to stay." Her voice was steel.

I ran towards the car. My lungs hurt from the cold and my feet slapped against the pavement. I was trying to think of things I could say to make him stay. My mother had stopped under a streetlamp to look for the car keys.

"Rufus." I stopped in front of them, out of breath. "Please stay." The cold air blew hair into my face. What am I doing? I thought.

Both of them looked at me, surprised.

"What's the matter?" she asked. Rufus stood with his cold breath around him and his hands in his pockets.

"Rufus, come on. It's about to start." That was Patricia, walking happily towards us like nothing was happening. "I have your ticket," she said.

My mother stepped away from him. "Just stay here," she said, opening the car door.

"Come on or we'll miss the trailers," Patricia said to Rufus. He was watching the car move slowly out of the parking spot.

"Come on," I said, and the three of us walked towards the cinema.

This is what mothers do: bend down to tie a shoelace, to wipe a mouth, wipe away tears, smooth down hair. Always looking over their shoulder. Standing at the edge of the pool: "Wear your water wings!" At the seaside: "Not too deep!" And now this, telling Rufus to stay here because her daughter asked, while she drives home alone through the dark and narrow roads to find her six-year-old son.

Inside, the cinema was warm: worn red rugs and the smell of butter and popcorn. They had Christmas decorations; silver tinsel streamers hung on the wall. I thought I could smell pine from the Christmas tree, but it was plastic. I measured myself against it, putting my hand on the top of my head and moving it in a straight line to the tree. The tree was a bit taller, but that was because of the star on top. I looked behind me to see if anyone was watching.

I had to touch the star; it was something I had to do. I touched one of the points with the tip of my finger. Something good will happen now, I thought.

It was a film about a dancer who hurts her foot, then recovers and wins a big contest. The woman in front of me had frizzy hair; I sat on my feet so I could see better but then my ankles hurt. I kicked the back of her chair, on purpose. I heard my mother say, "Why didn't you say something?" What if Eden had followed the cat outside to the rocks and had fallen? We'd find him in the morning, after we had been searching all night, lying like a rag doll by the shore.

At the back, a boy and girl were kissing. They would start and stop, making slurping sounds. During the film, Rufus climbed over me. Other people shuffled, standing up, moving their legs to the side so he could pass. I heard a man say, "Mind my foot!" When he crossed the projector you could see his shadow on the screen. Patricia watched him; her mouth went tight. He was gone for a long time, I thought maybe he was buying sweets, but he came back without any.

"That film made me feel like dancing," Annabel said, doing a shuffle forward and back as we walked out.

In the taxi, on the way back, Annabel kept trying to sing the theme song, "I'm gonna fly in the sky, high!" She threw her hands up with the song.

"You missed the best part, Rufus. Where did you go?" Patricia asked as we drove home.

"I went to phone Lucy to see if everything was all right."

"Was it?" Patricia asked.

"Eden's fine," he said.

"That was sweet of you," Patricia said. She put her hand on the back of his neck, massaging it, then lightly, just with the tips of her fingers. I knew what that felt like. Jolene and I did it to each other: the softest tickle. Rufus didn't look at her, he didn't tell her to stop; he let her move her fingers up and down the back of his neck as we rode home in the taxi.

When we were home and standing in the front hall with our coats still on, Patricia turned to Annabel and said, "Let's finish that wine upstairs."

"Yes, why don't we," Annabel said.

"Will you join us?"

"Okay," I said, nodding my head, and Annabel and Patricia laughed.

"We were talking to Rufus, darling."

"I'm actually quite tired," he said.

"Fine. More for us, then," Patricia said, and they started up the stairs to the sitting room.

My mother was in her room; I saw her through the open door, lying on her bed, eating something out of a teacup. I heard the sound of the spoon scraping against the cup. I walked right past her room without saying anything.

"May?"

I stopped but didn't turn around.

"May, come here." There was a picture on the wall, *A Spring Morning*. I stared at it, at the painted poppies, at the pale sky. I thought, I'm not going to say one word. For three days I won't say one word to her.

"May?" She stood outside her bedroom door. I stared at the picture, at the wooden frame. I put my finger in my mouth like I was biting my nails.

"May!" She shouted it.

"What?" I said it like she had surprised me.

"I just wanted to talk to you." She looked worried that I hadn't heard her.

"Oh." I looked at the picture again. "What are you eating?"

"Ice cream," she said. "Do you want some?"

I ran my finger over the moulding on the wall.

"Did you like the film?" she asked.

I looked down, like nothing could make me happy.

"I'm sorry I got cross with you about Eden."

I watched my fingers on the door. When I was little I pretended they were dancers; I played with them against the wall when I lay in bed waiting for my mother to wake up.

"I'm sorry, darling. I was worried. Come here."

I stood there twisting around on my feet.

"Don't you want some ice cream?"

I nodded my head but didn't move. I thought maybe I would take the bowl of ice cream and go to my room and not talk to her. That would be a mean thing to do.

"Come on, you silly child." She was almost laughing. She walked towards me and put her arm round my shoulder, patting me so I would smile. I didn't move. I made her do all the work. I tried not to smile, hunching my shoulders, dropping my chin, but I did anyway.

"Our favourite show is on," she said. It was a funny show about a detective. We walked into her room and sat down on the bed. "Do you want me to get you a bowl of ice cream?"

I nodded.

When she left the room I walked over to her dressing table and poked through her jewellery box. It was something I always did, opening the boxes, pulling out the drawers. It was mostly amber beads and Indian-looking jewellery, silver and turquoise. There was a hand-painted Russian box that had my baby teeth and an amethyst brooch that her mother had given to her when she was a child. Now there was something else in it: a small piece of paper. I took it out and unfolded it. It was the note Rufus had given her, written in another language. I refolded it and put it back in the box.

My mother came in holding two bowls of ice cream. She had stuck biscuits on top. There was a small telly on the bookcase. We piled up the pillows behind us on the bed and sat up watching, eating our bowls of ice cream. Like sisters.

...

We heard footsteps in the hall. We turned our heads to the door and a long shadow crossed over the wall; then Annabel walked in.

"Hello, darlings!" Annabel said. Her lips were a dark purple from the wine. "Where was he, your soppy son?"

"Sitting in his room with the cat."

"You missed the most wonderful movie. I should have been a dancer." She started waltzing around the room.

"Rufus phoned me from the theatre and said it wasn't very good actually—"

"Don't!" Annabel said, putting her hands over her ears.

It made me jump, the way she said it, loud and high. She stood like that, in the middle of the room, with her hands covering her ears. Then I laughed and so did my mother. It was something about her.

"What?" my mother asked.

Annabel opened her eyes and took a deep, loud breath. "Just don't get me started! I've wasted enough breath on him already. I tell you: Don't get me started."

My mother and I looked at her.

"You won't believe what he calls me behind my back," she said. "You won't bloody believe it!"

"What?" I asked loudly.

"What, Annabel?" my mother asked, holding her lips together, trying not to laugh.

"Mrs Bric-à-Brac!" Annabel said, holding her mouth open, acting shocked. "Can you believe it? The nerve, the bloody nerve!"

"Mrs Bric-à-Brac," my mother repeated, falling forward, turning bright red. Annabel started laughing too; she amused herself more than anyone else.

"If he only knew what I got for those Viennese figurines. I can just imagine his flat. It probably looks like a student's. A dusty old beanbag shoved in a corner. A bookshelf. What does he know about decorating? Some nerve, I tell you."

She kept making loud puffing sounds, like an impatient person having to wait in a long queue.

"Mrs Bric-à- . . ." my mother said, breathing in, sitting up, trying to say the whole thing without laughing, but then she would look at Annabel and start again, falling forward onto the bed and wiping her eyes.

Annabel sat on the small peach-coloured bedroom chair that my mother throws her clothes on. She held a shell in one hand for an ashtray and lit a cigarette with the other.

When my mother had calmed down, she looked at Annabel and asked, "Why are you looking at me like that, Annabel?"

I looked at Annabel too, sitting with her cigarette. She looked like there was something caught between her teeth.

"He's so funny," my mother said, taking a breath, her face still red from laughing.

"You wouldn't think he was so bloody funny if you'd heard what he said about you."

"What Rufus said about me?" my mother repeated slowly, sitting up straight, hugging her knees to her chest. She was serious now, not laughing.

Annabel looked around the room. "I need a cup of tea, darling, that wine's done my head in."

"What did he say about me?" my mother asked. Something in her voice sounded like the way Eden's had when he was in the middle of the lake for the first time with his water wings on. "I'm drifting! I'm drifting!" he screamed as he floated further away. Lost forever, alive but alone.

"Nothing, darling, I didn't mean to say anything. He's a bloody bore, really, and I'm not going to waste my breath. I'm not." She shook her head.

It was quiet in the room. No one spoke. My mother looked at Annabel and Annabel looked away. I stared at the telly. An old film was on.

"Isn't it time for Big Ears to go to bed?" Annabel asked. I had thought they would forget about me if I just lay very still.

"Yes, it is," my mother said.

"Can I sleep in here?" I still did sometimes, sleep in my mother's bed. My own room would be cold and everything would seem so still, the way a room felt when it was alone for a long time.

"Okay," my mother said. "But you have to brush your teeth."

I hurried out of the room and into the bathroom. My nightgown was still where I'd left it in the morning, on the floor by the sink. I brushed my teeth while I undressed, then ran back to my mother's room. I was pretending something was chasing me. I didn't want to miss anything. I knew they would keep talking. My mother would have to find out everything Rufus had said. She was that way about men: she asked a lot of questions but never did anything.

When I got back to the room they were gone. I stood in the doorway. The telly was off, the overhead light was off, and the blankets were turned down for me to get into bed.

I walked through the hazy dark room. The bed was still warm from where my mother and I sat, but it wasn't the same place it had been. I lay on my back with my eyes open. Everything swirled and shot past me, little things. I wasn't tired. Pieces of Annabel's voice came through the air. I held my breath but I couldn't hear whole words or sentences. Then I sat up. Outside, the trees looked bare and alone against the sky—that winter sky that's so heavy above you.

Then I did it. I couldn't help it, I was pulled out of bed and down the hall. I was barefoot, my feet were already cold. I held an empty glass in my hand. If I was caught, I would just be on my way to the kitchen for a drink. Not water, I could get that from any sink. I wanted milk, apple juice, or Ribena.

The kitchen door was closed. I leaned against the wall next to it. Annabel's voice was louder than my mother's; it came straight at me. I had to strain, holding my breath, to hear my mother.

"Oh, it's obvious," Annabel said.

Obvious is one of those words, like a slap. Like when you aren't looking and then suddenly someone throws something that hits you in the head.

"What's obvious?" my mother asked.

"That you fancy him, darling."

Now my mother was like me in the swimming pool, right after they pulled off my bikini top and dragged it through the water, the straps floating behind like an octopus. Right then, when you put your hands across your chest, when you try to hide yourself, but everyone can see. Everyone can tell, he can see, he can see.

"I do not fancy him. We've become quite good friends since he's been here, Annabel, that's all."

"Well, he doesn't sound like a very nice friend," Annabel said.

Then there was a *pop*. It was the electric kettle; the water was done.

"Quick, darling, quick!" Annabel was shooing my mother. "Make me a cup of tea. Strong, not a pissy little cup."

"Why doesn't he sound like a very nice friend?" my mother asked, imitating the way Annabel had said "nice".

There were noises, chairs moving, footsteps back and forth. I thought one of them might suddenly open the door. What if they had to pee? I took a step back.

"If you must know . . . and I'm only telling you for your own good, so you'll know. Like the time when that Mary Foster found my journal and read it to all the girls during lunch. I always wondered why they looked at me like that; *you* knew and didn't tell me. . . . I always think it's better to tell," Annabel said. I had heard this story before. It was probably Annabel's worst memory, and she held it over my mother's head like a rock.

"I know, Annabel. I'm sorry, I should have told you." My mother sounded tired. It had happened years ago, when they were at school together.

"It's okay, Lucy," Annabel said softly, as though she were finally forgiving her.

Everything was silent for a moment.

"What did he say about me?"

I slid down against the wall. Everything was always about men.

"Well, he told Patricia that it was hard for him to get much work done here because you were always asking him to do things . . . and—well, he just feels a bit uncomfortable."

"He feels uncomfortable?" My mother's voice was moving very slowly. "Why?"

"I don't know, darling . . . because of the way you act towards him. He thinks you have the hots for him. . . . Don't worry. He's probably the type of man who thinks everyone is flirting with him . . . and I don't know why, what with that wonky leg of his."

"But, *he's* the one who's always coming up here asking *me* to do things. . . . You can ask May." That startled me. I thought I should run back to bed. But I knew Annabel wouldn't ask me. She wasn't interested in the truth; she was just telling my mother what she'd heard from Patricia.

"I believe you, darling," Annabel said. "You were probably just being friendly. You know how men are, they think everything is a come-on. Anyway, he'll be gone soon enough. Patricia told me they want to get back to London and have some time to themselves before Christmas."

"Oh, good," my mother said. I heard her put a cup down on the saucer. "Good. Because to tell you the truth I can't stand either of them, especially her. I really don't know why you like her."

"Don't get angry with me, Lucy. You wanted to know—I knew this would happen—you asked me to tell you."

"Did she say anything else?" my mother asked. It's important to know everything; that's how you unravel it.

"I'm not talking about this any more," Annabel said.

"Tell me if she said anything else." My mother sounded as though she was becoming very cold. As though she was walking home in the winter, in the rain, when you become so cold you can see the blue veins under your skin.

"No. She didn't say anything else, Lucy."

I went back to my own room. When I pulled the blankets over me, I thought I could hear Rufus and Patricia downstairs, their laughter rising up and up, roaring, louder and louder, like a furnace.

That night different sounds woke me: a creak in the floorboards, the click of a light switch, the running tap. It was my mother, walking through the house and in circles around her room, pressing the palms of her hands tightly together in front of her, like a prayer.

Fourteen

I woke up early the next morning. It was a bright day, that white bright when the sun is right behind the clouds, trying, almost coming through. I sat up in bed. I was awake right away; sometimes that happens. Suddenly, one morning, you wake up with the energy of summer. I opened the paper door on the advent calendar that my grandmother had sent me; inside were three lighted candles. I listened to see if anyone else was awake. It was quiet in the house that morning; nothing moved. I walked down the hall. My mother's bedroom door was open, her side of the bed was still made, the blankets pulled up over the pillows. The side I had been in was still the same, the blankets pulled down. The empty ice cream bowl was on the floor.

Eden's bedroom door was closed, she was probably in there, asleep on one of the twin beds, side by side with a lamp shaped like a propeller aeroplane between them. She does that, goes to another bed in the middle of the night when she can't sleep. Sometimes she sleeps in one of the guest rooms and then the next day she has to change the sheets if someone's coming. Folding them down, tucking them tightly into the corners.

The kitchen was having its own tea party. Everything was left on the table. The pink teapot and two cups on saucers, filled with tea. The bottle of milk was right in the middle of the table with its top lying next to it, like a fallen hat. There was an ashtray and a packet of round chocolate-covered biscuits. The sun came in through the windows.

There was another cup on the counter, a mug from last night with a camomile tag hanging over the side, like a small flag. I think they're pretty, tea tags. I put my hand around the mug. It was still warm.

From the window you could see the sea and the rocks and the tops of the trees. Everything seemed very still; only the sea swayed forward and back, forward and back, like an old woman in a rocking chair. It's almost Christmas and it looks like a summer day. I put my hand on the windowpane, pressed flat against it. It was like nothing, like touching your own skin.

...

Annabel was sitting up in bed holding a cup of tea over the saucer, sponge rollers in a dance around her head. She put time into getting ready every day, even in the country.

"Good morning." She didn't turn her head to look at me, she just moved her eyes to the side, over her teacup. I walked over to the bed. There was a dark blue light in the room; the curtains were still drawn shut.

"Darling, open the curtains." I stood between the long blue curtains and pulled them apart as though they were a pair of heavy wet wings.

She shaded her eyes with her hand. It wasn't that bright, but that's what she was like in the morning. She wore a black T-shirt that had the words 14 CARAT GOLD AND WORTH IT printed on it in glittery gold letters.

"What's on your face?" I asked. It was all shiny.

"Vaseline." She was looking into her tea.

"Oh."

"You put it on before you go to bed, and in the morning you wake up looking moist and fresh. I forgot to put it on last night, so I did it this morning. Patricia told me about it, but don't tell anyone else." Annabel didn't want anyone else to wake up looking moist and fresh.

"Can I tell Mum?" I just wanted to see.

"She knows. God forbid she put some effort into herself! How long have I been telling her to get highlights? She *has* been dressing a bit better, I must admit."

Annabel puffed the pillows up behind her and began to undo each sponge roller from her hair with a sulky yank. They made her hair fall straight, then curl up underneath perfectly.

"There's a Christmas sale at the church next to my school today."

"A sale? A sale?" Her teacup froze in the air; her body stiffened with excitement.

...

The jumble sale smelled of moss. In the church cellar, ladies from this town and others nearby sat on metal fold-up chairs next to their tables of goods: hand-knitted baby sweaters and tea cosies, loo-paper covers, and jars of jams wrapped in cloth. Annabel still had the Vaseline on her face, so I walked behind her. There was a round table with a few chairs to sit on where they sold scones and tea. We stopped for a cup. There was a long row of picnic tables covered in piles of scrambled clothes.

We drank our tea and waited for the man with the china to finish setting up his table. He had been irritated earlier when Annabel hovered over him, watching, as he unwrapped each piece from its newspaper.

"These are the only places you can find anything nowadays, especially now the dealers know about you-know-who," she whispered to me over her cup of tea.

I shook my head. My mouth full of scone. She was talking about Clarice Cliff; Annabel collected her china and, since she began, so has everybody else in London. Every woman wanted a piece of it in her kitchen. People are like that; they all want the same things.

"Now, most of this is just crap, but occasionally you find something gorgeous." Last time Annabel was here she found a honeycomb butter dish. Her eyes moved slowly over each table. Spotting a woman approaching the man with the china she put her tea down. "Quick, quick!" she said, pulling me up by the sleeve and over to the table. "Remember what to look for."

Wedgwood, Staffordshire, Shelley teapots, and Cliff.

"Don't be obvious." She nudged me with her elbow as I stood holding a floral plate upside down.

There was a girl, I think she was twenty, with a long face and dark red hair sitting at the table next to us. In front of her were piles of lace knickers and bras in all different colours and sizes. She was reading a book, carefully turning the pages. Women gathered around the table, picking up bras and holding the knickers up to their waists. She put the book down open on her lap, folded her hands over it, and looked up. I thought, I would be embarrassed to sit here with these women and their cakes and jams, at a table of lacy things. But she was just sitting there, letting people look, pick things up, drop them down.

I checked to make sure Annabel was not near and walked towards the bras. I wanted to hold one, but I was surrounded by mothers. I slid my fingers over the closest one to me, on the edge of the table.

"Oh, purple for passion," someone said to me. It was the woman who looked like a witch, the one I had overheard talking about me in front of Barbara Whitmore's mother. My face went cold and I put the bra back.

Annabel walked towards me with a brown jug in one hand and a green sweater tucked under her arm.

"One hundred per cent pure cashmere, darling! Guess how much?" I had seen her pull it out from underneath another woman's pile on the clothes table. I shrugged; my fingers shook.

"Fifty pence! Can you believe it? I could have probably got it for less." She held it up. It was a green cardigan with embroidered yellow flowers around the neck and wrists.

"I'll give it to your mother for Christmas, she likes this kind of thing. The country look, the 'I have just come from the vegetable patch' look."

...

When we got home there was a red car parked in front of the house, a small zippy bright-red car. Annabel drove towards it slowly, peering through the front window.

"What is that?" she said, as she stepped out of the car.

"Someone must be here," I said.

"That is naff," she said. We stood side by side looking at the car. "He's probably French and likes very young girls. He might even like you."

It was the brightest thing around; none of the summer guests drove cars like it. It looked as though there was only room for one man and a thin woman next to him, with a purse on her lap.

"How do you know it's a man's car?"

Annabel looked at me blank-faced. "I know."

The kind of man who would wear a short fur jacket, who would take a step back if a cat or dog came too near his trousers: that kind of man.

"At least we know one good thing about him," Annabel said.
"What?"

"He's rich," she said, and ran up the stairs to wash the Vaseline off, which she told me takes a very long time but is worth it. "It's a poor man's face-lift."

There was a square brown suitcase by the front door, I bent down to read the tag but there was nothing written on it. I smelled something, wood and soap. It reminded me of something; I had smelled it before on a man's neck. I have secretly searched for it in other people's houses, locking the bathroom door, smelling all the soaps and things in bottles.

It made me hungry, and I walked upstairs to the kitchen. I could hear my mother talking to someone; the door was open. She was talking to a man, I could see the back of his head. A long neck, thin for a man, dark hair, wavy and brushed back. A cup of tea on a saucer next to him, he leaned on his elbow and stirred and stirred with a small spoon. I could hear the tinkling sound it made against the side of the cup.

My mother was wiping the long pepper grinder with a yellow cloth. I thought, I know him! When my mother lifted her head, to ask if he wanted sugar or honey, she saw me standing by the side of the door and stared at me. He noticed and turned around to look.

It was him. His green eyes, like my green eyes. It was my father.

"May, look who's here. Come and say hello." Her voice was high and strained. I thought I should jump up and shout "Dad!" but I was too surprised. I didn't have time to act the way I had always planned to when this happened.

My father sat at the table with his cup of tea. I thought he would stand up, pick me up and kiss me, swing me around, but he just sat there stirring his tea.

I stepped into the kitchen like a prisoner, my arms at my sides. My hands felt hot and itchy. I walked over and kissed him on the cheek. He brought one hand up around the back of my neck and the other around my waist and pulled me onto his lap, like a baby. I tried to laugh and act ticklish, but the sound that came out sounded more like a squeak and made me blush.

"You've got bigger," he said. His hand rested on my stomach. I held it in. My mother always told me he liked thin girls.

...

The last time I saw him was three years ago at my birthday party in London. I was turning nine and had paper plates with flower fairies on them. I saved a place for him next to me and put the party hat with the real blue feather on his chair. It was the best one. I watched the clock on the wall, and every sound near the door made me start. When he finally showed up the party was almost over, but he had a beautifully wrapped box under his arm, store-wrapped, with even folds and clear tape. It was from the ballet store where everything is the colour of roses and made with thick stitches. Inside the box were soft pink slippers, shiny and new, with that square rounded toe I loved.

I wanted to put them on right away, but when my mother saw them something in her face fell. She whispered to me to try them on later because the other girls might get jealous. Annabel and Suzy were there, and a friend of Eden's so they could play together. Later, when I tried, I couldn't get my heel into the slippers. They were too small. When we went to return them that weekend, the thin saleswoman in a tartan skirt held them up and looked them over, inspecting. Finally, she handed them back to us and said, "We haven't carried this brand in a year or two. They're old stock."

...

"Are you hungry?" my mother asked. Her voice was tight. I could tell she needed me.

"No." I was before but now it was gone. The warmth from my father's neck and the smell was turning my face red. Suddenly he was bored and made a sound like a yawn. He put his hand between my shoulders and slowly pushed me off his lap. I got stuck between him and the table and wasn't sure whether I was supposed to sit on his lap again or if he had meant me to move away. I walked towards the sink. I needed to put cold water on my face.

Eden was sitting under the table. He had his legs pulled up to his chest and his arms wrapped around them.

"What's he doing?" I asked my mother. It was strange to speak in front of my father. My voice sounded like it was hardly there.

"I don't know." She looked tired, the way people do when they're trying to walk quickly down a crowded street. "You all right under there?"

She bent over and gave him a little poke in the back. He dropped his head down between his knees, like a hopeless dog.

"What did I do wrong?" She was talking about Eden. It made him squirm and bang his hand down on the floor. She looked at my father and raised her eyebrows as if to say: Tell me something. Do you know why my son is sitting under the table with his arms wrapped around his knees? But he only shrugged and pulled out a cigarette from a wide blue box. There were matches on the table, red-tipped safety matches; he ignored them, stood up, and walked out of the kitchen. He took a few steps down the hall to the coat rack, looked in his pockets, and reappeared holding a thin gold lighter.

I watched him walk across the room. He was handsome, that was the first thing anyone ever said about him. My grandmother has a friend named Lady Willoughby de Brook whose voice is so high and pink it's like a song. We had lemon tea in her garden once, and she tried to explain to my grandmother. "You know what he's got? Sex appeal."

I heard slow footsteps in the hall. I looked out and saw Annabel checking herself in the mirror. She walked in with her head high, then stopped stiff when she saw him.

"Don't tell me! It's not!" She had her hand on her chest and her mouth open in an exaggerated gasp. She was the funniest person I knew.

"Hello, darling," he said, getting up to hug her. He looked alive at last. They had the same voice. They were both from the East End but had moved into the Chelsea crowd, so now there was a higher ring to it. My grandmother called it *raffinée*.

"To what do we owe this visit?" she asked, with her hands on her hips.

"You're all dressed up, darling, got a date with a farmer?" Her hair was blown straight with an under curl, a classic look but also chic; that's what she told me.

"Believe me, if I'd known it was just you I wouldn't have bothered. Did you bring us any goodies?"

"He did bring up some kippers," my mother said. She was more relaxed now that everyone was in the room.

"So we can cook for him, thank you very much. I hope they're from Harrods' food hall," Annabel said. She loved visitors, especially men.

...

The beach here is not wide or as long as ribbons, like the one on the postcards my grandmother sends from Rhode Island, America. There are large rocks that stretch into the sea like lions' claws, and in between are patches of sand. So to walk on the beach you have to climb, with one leg up and a bent back, hands on the rocks.

There was my father in his trousers and slippery black shoes. He'd asked me in the kitchen if I wanted to take a walk with him. We hadn't gone very far when he sat down for a cigarette, the end of our walk. Before he sat down he asked for my jacket to sit on so he wouldn't mark his trousers. I was warm and had tied it around my waist. It was my favourite electric-blue corduroy. Annabel said it brought out the colour in my eyes; that's why I'd worn it. I handed it to him as though I didn't care, but when he sat on it I felt like I was being squashed.

It had been a bright morning, but now the clouds were coming in. My father sat with his knees up, staring at the sea. "It's quite nice here, you know."

I was standing behind him. "It's nice." I kicked the top of my plimsoll against the rock.

"Come and sit over here, I'm not going to bite," he said. I sat down cross-legged. Underneath me felt like a cold metal swing. I left a space between us, big enough for another person to sit. My stomach was making noises.

"Your car is nice," I said.

"Thanks," he said, looking out, smoking his cigarette.

Beneath us the waves splashed against the rocks. I retied my shoelace, to have something to do. It was beginning to get cold, and I was hungry. But nothing mattered at that moment. I would have sat through the rain, through the night. I only wanted one thing: for him to like me.

"So there's not much business in the winter then?" he asked.

"Hardly anyone comes, but there are two people here right now."

"Two people." He made a puffing sound like it was nothing, pathetic. "See, I'll tell you something. I've found this great little piece of property in south London"—he was gesturing with his hands—"an old building, like a house." He made a house with his hands. "I'm going to turn it into a food and wine bar."

"Yeah," I said, so he knew I was listening.

"It's a good idea, if I do say so myself. You could move back to London. We could see more of each other. I mean, it's such a schlep up here. . . ."

"Are you staying for Christmas?" This happens; I get ahead of myself, excited. But he had started it; he said it first. He said we could get to see more of each other.

He nodded, looking out. "I might," he said slowly, still nodding. Then he turned and looked back towards the house. "It's a little bleak here. Not a very cheerful place, is it?"

In the kitchen when he'd asked me to go on a walk, I thought he was going to tell me something, a secret about me. I thought, This will be an important moment on the rocks, alone with my father. More than anything else, I was flattered.

"I fancy a cup of tea," he said, getting up, handing me back my damp, briny jacket.

We walked back together side by side, the sea so quiet and constant it was like the air. The only sound was the gravel under our shoes. This will be a real memory, I thought.

When we were nearer the house I saw something: the end of someone disappeared around the side of the house. I looked at my father to see if he'd seen it too, but he was looking at the roof, inspecting, sizing it up, in the way that he did. The way you look at something you might buy.

Then he stopped suddenly. "Come here a minute, will you?" I walked over to where he stood, and he placed his hand on my shoulder. I stood very still. I couldn't breathe all the way. I could hear something, like a horse's trot, coming towards us.

"I've got something caught in my shoe," he said. He leaned his weight on me and stood on one foot. He pulled his shoe off.

His sock was thin, a silvery colour. No holes. He held his shoe carefully in his hand, like the glass slipper. Then he turned it upside down and something fell out—there was a *clink*—a small stone, a piece of gravel.

The sound was louder, the trotting sound coming towards us. I looked to where it was coming from. Then I saw what it was: Patricia, doing her jog around the house. She ran towards us in her pink leotard, her short hair flopping up and down.

"Hi!" she yelled to us.

My father stopped and looked at her, running towards us, waving with one hand. Then she stopped right in front of us but kept moving up and down, jogging in place.

"Hi, May," she said again. Her cheeks were pink. She seemed happy, like when you get ready for something.

"This is my father," I said loudly, so she would know. Now she would see I had a handsome father from London. Now she would know we didn't care about Rufus or what he said about us. I wished he were holding my hand.

"You're May's father?" Her leotard was a thin pale pink, almost see-through, the colour of skin.

"I'm Simon." He put out his hand.

"Patricia." She smiled at him. "May's told me about you." Something inside me stopped. I thought, Don't say that, don't tell him. I felt as though those words were being carved inside me. I twisted the button on my coat.

When I looked up, Patricia was smiling at me.

"She is a very sweet girl."

"She'll be pretty when she gets those teeth fixed," my father said, laughing. My hand went up to my mouth, quickly; it hit me on the lips. I'd forgotten about my teeth until just now; they were a little crooked on the side.

"Don't worry, I had to wear braces for years when I was young," Patricia said.

"There's hope," my father said, and patted me on the head. But it hurt; his hand was heavy. Then they both laughed.

"Are you staying for a while?" she asked, kicking her legs up high behind her.

"Yeah, I might do."

"Are you still going to do my hair for Barbara's party?" I wanted him to know we were friends.

"Of course I will, May," she said, and ran off on her jog again.

He stood there, we both did, looking after her.

"Great legs," he said.

"She's here with her boyfriend," I told him.

"So?" he said, looking at me like he didn't understand. "She's still got great legs."

We walked together, towards the house.

...

"Make me a cup a tea, will you?" my father said, as he walked into the living room and switched on the telly.

"Do you want me to put sugar or honey in it?" He was moving the aerial around, adjusting it to the perfect position.

On the telly, men in tight shorts ran around kicking a ball.

"Two," he said, staring at the telly.

He must have meant sugar. I knew he meant sugar, but I wanted to make sure.

"Two sugars?" I asked. He was leaning forward with his hands on his knees, his nose almost touching the screen.

There was a note on the kitchen table. It read:

Dear Simon and May,
I'm taking a bath. May, Jolene phoned. She said you were
supposed to be at her house to go Christmas shopping.

I looked up at the clock on the wall. It was past two. I had forgotten we were going Christmas shopping today. I looked back at the note on the table, at my father's name next to mine. He's really here, I thought. I folded the note in squares and put it in my pocket.

I made the tea twice; the first time it didn't look dark enough. I measured the sugar, flattening my finger over the spoon so it was exactly a teaspoonful, then stirred it in. I took a tiny sip, testing it, and afterward I wiped the place where my mouth had been with a napkin. I brought it to him on a saucer, walking slowly, making sure the tea didn't sway over the edge.

He was lying down on the sofa with his feet on the armrest. I handed him his tea.

"Just leave it on the table," he said. My hands shook as I bent over and set it down; it clinked and wobbled but nothing spilled. His shoes were tucked neatly together under the table. He started pushing his hand through the air, the way you try to get a fly, a mosquito, away from you. Finally, he said in a loud voice, "Move!" Then I realized it was me; I was in the way, standing between him and the telly.

I can be slow like that sometimes. Things will happen around me and I won't notice them. I took a ballet class once, and we were all lined up on the floor doing our stretches. But the next time I looked up, everyone was at the bar doing pliés and I was still sitting on the floor.

Loud music and cheers came from the television; a checkered ball flew across the field. There was no room on the sofa; he lay right across it, his head resting on one arm and his feet up on the other.

The chair I sat on was peach-coloured with butterflies embroidered on it. They were all different. I traced their wings with my finger, trying to find my favourite, which one I would want to be.

The sound of the telly was hurting my head. I pressed the palm of my hand against my forehead. It felt hot. I remembered that I had to phone Jolene. My father sat up and I thought, Good, we'll do something else now. I'll show him my room.

"Hand me my coat, will you, babes?" He put his hand in the coat pocket and pulled out a small box. It was an old throat lozenge tin. My grandmother always had them in her handbag; they were gummy and tasted of black currants. From the box he took out rolling papers and matches. He lit a match and held what looked like a dark brown stone up to the flame, warming it; then he crumbled it over the tobacco, wrapped it tightly in the paper, licked the edge and smoothed it closed. He stared at the telly, leaning forward, and lit it with his gold lighter. Thick white smoke went all around him.

When the game was over, he said, "I told your mum that I'd take you two out for a really nice meal tonight. So dress up a little, look smart."

I ran down the hall. Things are changing, things are changing. My father's here from London; the world is coming to me. I thought, He can take me to Barbara's party.

I ran a bath, but only filled it halfway, so there would be enough hot water for him, my father. I used my new lavender soap. I had one fancy dress, the one my grandmother gave me last Christmas. Deep red velvet with a white collar but it looked old-fashioned, too old-fashioned for him.

When I looked at my teeth in the mirror, I wished I had the kind of toothpaste that makes your teeth white. I practised smiling with my mouth closed, but then I remembered that Patricia had "whitening tooth polish". I'd seen it on her sink.

I dressed and went downstairs. My hair was still wet, dripping down my back.

I could hear the radio coming from Patricia's room when I knocked on the door. She was lying on her bed, looking through a magazine, her ankles crossed in front of her.

"What are you doing?" I asked. She was wearing a scoop-neck T-shirt dress with miniature pink hearts on it. There was a pile of cards in green envelopes next to her.

"Writing my Christmas cards. I was halfway through my list when I got bored."

A fire was burning in the fireplace. She tapped her toes to the music and turned the pages of her magazine.

"I love this coat. Oh, God! I want this coat." She was pointing to one of the models. I walked over to look. "Your dad's handsome. What does he do again?" she asked, moving her eyes to look at me.

"He works in London at a business." It sounded wrong after I said it. So I said, "But he's going to open a wine bar."

"A wine bar? That'll be nice." She turned over on her side and rested her head on her hand.

"Does Rufus still want you to leave?" I asked, just so she knew I remembered.

Her smile went and her body looked stiff.

"No, and he never really did. It was all a big misunderstanding, May." Then she smiled at me in that way again, wide and big like a gate.

"Can I use your toothpaste?"

"My toothpaste?" She sat up cross-legged on the bed.

"I saw it in here before. The kind that makes your teeth whiter. My father's taking us out to dinner." That's all I had to tell her—she would understand wanting to look good.

"You're going out to dinner? Is your mum going too?"

I nodded.

"May, I know! I know!" she said, jumping up. "I'll blow-dry your hair and put some blusher and shadow on you. You'll look gorgeous!"

"But what can we do about these front bits?" I tugged at my overgrown fringe, the one I'd cut myself. I acted like this, a little bit sulky, so she would want to help me more.

She jumped up and went into the bathroom, humming along with the song on the radio. It was easy to see why men liked her, why Annabel liked her, why anyone would. Everything she did seemed like fun. I couldn't imagine her tired, dragging a cloth across the kitchen table.

There were rows of different-coloured lipsticks and nail polishes on her dresser. She held a spray bottle in one hand, a hair dryer in the other, and sat me down in front of the mirror. She brushed my hair, starting at the ends, the way my mother does, so the knots don't pull at my head. See, I thought, she is nice. There were other things on her dresser—a little blue china box tied with a white china ribbon, like a present. I lifted the top. Inside was a thin diamond cross on a gold chain.

She wrapped my hair around the hairbrush and pulled it straight out, away from my head. Then she pointed the dryer at it and turned it on high. She was still humming the same song from before. I looked at myself in the mirror. I liked the way I looked with my hair wet and flat against my face. My eyes looked big, like something new.

There was a knock on the door, I heard it through the blow dryer.

"Hold this." She switched it off and dropped it on my lap.

"Did you just get back? You must be exhausted," I heard her say. Her voice sounded different, softer.

I turned to look. Rufus was standing in the doorway in his coat and brown woolen hat.

"I thought you were going back to London," he said to her in a low voice, almost a whisper. His face looked long, fallen.

"I'm just doing May's hair. Her father's come down from London, and he's taking Lucy and her out to a fancy dinner." Hearing it made it sound real, like a present I could hold in my hands.

Rufus looked at me from the doorway.

"Did you get lots of work done?" she asked again, in that kind of birdlike voice.

"So, are you leaving tomorrow?" he asked her. It sounded like any other question, just a little shorter.

He walked past her towards me, where I sat in front of the mirror.

"Your father came? Your father or Eden's?" That was Rufus, standing near me with his hands in his pockets, his hair messy from his hat. Asking because he wanted her to know that he knew things about us, things my mother told him. Everyone else thought Eden and I had the same father.

"*My* father," I said, as though it were the beginning and the end. My father, Amen.

"Oh." He looked down at his feet, nodding long, slow nods, up and down. "Is he staying here?"

"He's come for Christmas," I said. He looked away from me and sat down on the edge of the bed.

Patricia came over, carrying a handful of lime-green plastic curlers. She separated my hair into thin pieces and wrapped it around them, so it would go under at the ends. It pinched in places but I sat still.

"Lucy seems so happy now that he's here. She looks radiant," Patricia said, turning slightly towards the bed, where Rufus sat looking down at his hands.

She turned the dryer on, holding it close to my head. It felt like it was burning my scalp, turning it red. I wrapped my hands around the sides of the chair and counted to ten. It will be done then, I said. But she just stood there holding the dryer in one hand, her other hand on her hip. I tried to think of cool things, like swimming, to make the burning stop. I remembered Annabel saying, "You have to suffer to be beautiful."

"Have you seen Lucy?" Rufus asked loudly from the bed.

"Mmm-hmm," Patricia said. She turned off the dryer and leaned over me as she put it down on the dresser. She smelled of something sweet.

"Lucy told me she didn't . . ." he stopped himself, remembering I was there, but I knew what he had been going to say—"that they don't get along."

"Really?" Patricia asked, her voice going up. She took a tall metal bottle and sprayed it around my head. It smelled like bug spray. "Annabel told me she thought Lucy would always be in love with him. That's what it's like with your first love; you never really get over it."

Her voice was loud in my ear, but she wanted it to reach him on the bed.

She picked up the dryer to finish, quicker now, pulling harder. I heard the door shut, and when I looked back Rufus was gone. When she was done, my hair fell around my head softly, like a silk scarf. The blond streaks left over from the summer looked brighter. I moved my head from side to side. My hair swung back and forth, then landed neatly against my shoulders.

...

Annabel was in the kitchen with Eden, making him dinner.

"Don't mind me, I'm just the nanny tonight. Nanny Annabel! Right, Eden?" He nodded his head, his mouth full of something white and doughy, a piece of cake.

"Your hair looks nice, darling! Very sophisticated."

My mother came in, clasping a beaded earring to one ear. She looked taller. It was her shoes, black suede with a small heel. She wore a tight rose-coloured crocheted top and a black velvet skirt that went to her knees, with a long slit up the side, her hair in a loose twist.

"I hope you two have a good time. Don't bother about me, I'll just be here with my friend Eden, watching a bit of telly and reading *Mother Hubbard*," Annabel said, waving goodbye to us.

My mother walked down the stairs slowly, pulling up her stockings. Her shirt sparkled under the light.

"Maybe I should just run downstairs and check on the heat. It gets so cold down there."

"Okay," I said, smoothing down the front of my dress.

She looked down the hallway. She wanted Rufus to see her, dressed up like this, but he wasn't there. No one ever sees you when you want them to.

My father was already outside, wiping his car down with a cloth.

"Look at you two, don't you look lovely?" He moved his eyes up and down my mother. He was wearing a wide-collared shirt under a tweed jacket that was tight in the waist and grey trousers with turn-ups.

"I'm taking my girls out to dinner," he said, opening the only door on the passenger side, making a half bow and swinging his arm out like the men do with a red cloth in front of the bulls. There was no seat in the back. There was no back at all, just a tiny corner under the sloped top.

"There's really no room for her back there," my mother said, looking back at me. It was like lying under a bed. My head pressed up against the side.

"She's fine," my father said. I nodded, but my neck hurt.

"No. It's too dangerous. She can sit on my lap, and we'll put the seat belt across both of us."

"It'll make the car look crowded," he told her. His mouth went tight.

"So?" My mother kept looking towards the house. I was afraid we'd never get to the restaurant.

"Let's take my car," she said. I saw him turn his head slowly, looking it over.

"All right, just bung her on your bloody lap then." He got in the car and slammed the door behind him.

Fifteen

The restaurant was in the Red Lion Hotel. The tables were covered with ironed white tablecloths, one red candle in the middle, next to a silver thimble of salt with a tiny doll's spoon and a silver pepper grinder. Two brass chandeliers hung from the ceiling; heavy red velvet curtains surrounded the windows; a fire burned in an old brick fireplace. It was warm and full of dressed-up people, sitting up straight, holding glasses of wine.

A man in a black suit led us to a round table in the back. My father stopped him just as he was pulling out a chair. "We would prefer to sit at a banquette."

I thought, What is that, a banquette? The waiter tucked the menus under his arm and quickly led us to one of the long tables with cushioned benches that lined the back wall.

My mother squeezed in, then my father, and I sat across from them on an ordinary wooden chair. The menus were long, written in black script, too much to read. I couldn't concentrate. I was going to order a Coca-Cola: we were never allowed it at home; it was a treat, something for restaurants.

My father looked around, nodding in approval. "Not bad, not too bad for the country," he said to us. My mother seemed tired, lost next to the dark wooden wall. She yawned and brought her hand to her mouth.

"Why are you so tired?" I asked. It made me angry that she was tired tonight, with him, in this restaurant. I wanted her to be fun.

The waiter put down a basket of white rolls and a plate full of thin curls of butter on sprinkles of ice. They looked like white shells, ridged and curved. I took a roll; it was still warm.

"Do you work on a farm?" my father asked across the table from me, low and rough. I looked up at him. I thought it was the beginning of a joke.

"What?"

"Your fingernails." He pointed with his little finger, his pinky; there was a gold ring on it.

The roll was between my hands on the small plate, almost broken. I looked down and saw dirt under my nails.

"Why don't you go and scrub them before we eat our meal?" He picked up the small silver spoon and tapped it lightly, so that a few grains of salt sprinkled over the butter on his roll.

"It's just country dirt," my mother told him, sitting up, putting her napkin on her lap. I couldn't see her face clearly; a shadow fell over her.

I got up from the table and went to find the loo. I kept my fingers curled into my palms so the waiter wouldn't see. "To the back and down the stairs," the waiter told me. He had blondish-red hair and skin that looked like dough. I thought he was nineteen. He gave me the directions like a palace guard. His shoes were old but shiny, trying to look new, tricking everyone, unless you looked at the heels.

When I came back to the table, my father was ordering a bottle of wine from the red-haired waiter. I thought my father was going to take my hand, spread my fingers out to inspect, but he didn't.

After he ordered the wine, he turned to my mother, who was buttering a piece of her roll, and said, "I was telling May about it earlier when I took her for a walk."

"She's not a dog," my mother said.

"What?" He looked at her, a little startled.

I held my lips tight in a smile so I wouldn't laugh. My mother looked over at me and smiled too. You couldn't laugh at him; he wasn't that type of man. It would make him angry.

"Telling me about what?" I asked. He kept looking at my mother, talking very slowly, like each word he said was a piece of gold.

"I found this little house," he said. We both stared at him with very serious expressions. "Beautiful, an old carriage house. Fred is going to be my partner on the premises, help me handle things. We've found some very prominent backers: Keith Richards, Ozzy Clark. That will attract an exclusive crowd." He put a cigarette between his lips and lit it. "We want it to be the new place. Not just anyone can come in, only if you know someone."

"That sounds fantastic, Simon." She said it in one flat line, like a wooden board.

"We're thinking of calling it Dandelions."

The waiter came and took our order. He didn't write it down, just locked it away until he reached the kitchen.

"I was thinking I would give you an opportunity to be one of the main investors—you know, before the word gets out and everyone wants a piece. It's going to be a great place, really fabulous, only the best beer and wine and some little savouries."

"Savouries?"

"Escargots and things. No chips."

"It sounds really great," she said.

He nodded, and touched the top of his hair lightly.

"But I don't have any money to invest. You know that."

I squeezed my toes under the table, I hated it when she said that. It seemed like we could fall right over the edge. No money.

The waiter held a bottle of wine with a white napkin wrapped around it. He poured a drop into my father's glass. My father lifted the glass by the stem and held it to the light, then stuck his nose over the glass as though he were about to dive in, sniffed it, then sipped it. It took a long time. The waiter watched, waiting.

Finally my father nodded at his glass. "Quite nice, actually," he said, and something soft settled in his face, a small white feather falling through the air, rocking to the ground.

The waiter poured the wine, but my father stopped him with his hand when the glasses were half-filled. And the waiter, carrying the wine in both hands, walked away from our table.

He looked at me and said, "Darling daughter, will you pass me a roll?" He put on a fake upper-class accent, making his face long. I handed him the roll with my clean fingernails. He took my hand and bent over to kiss the top of it like a prince, but instead he kissed the top of his own hand. It was the first time anyone had done this to me, and I laughed the way I have seen women laugh at men's jokes: a little louder, a little longer, touching them on the shoulder—but I couldn't do that, I was too far away across the table. My mother sat forward a little, into the light. I could see her face now; her cheeks were red from the wine. She had finished her glass already.

He started showing me a trick. He held his hands out in front of me and pretended to take his thumb off, then put it back. He had shown me this trick before, when I was little, and it had looked so real I made him do it over and over again. I didn't want him to have a missing thumb, it made me feel sorry for him. But now I knew how he did this trick, it didn't look real to me any more. I could even do it myself, but still I asked him to do it again, saying, "How do you do that?" to make him think he hadn't missed that much, that things hadn't really changed since the last time I saw him. I was a few inches taller, a few years older. He could use the same trick forever, and I would never figure it out.

Our food came on big white plates with a thin gold band around the edge, steaming. I had shepherd's pie. The potatoes on top were a crispy gold, but too hot to eat right away. If I had been alone with my mother, I would have picked off the top part with my fingers, waiting for the rest to cool. Instead, I sat up straight with my hands in my lap.

"You're a great conversationalist tonight, Lucy," he said to my mother in a sarcastic voice, as he cut into his roast beef. She squeezed lemon over her fish, not looking at him. "I can't get a word in edgewise."

I laughed at everything he said.

"I'm tired," she said, pushing her hair behind her ears. She looked like she was trying to remember something, the way I sit over my maths book, trying to figure it out, to solve the problems.

"Who are you dating these days?" my mother asked him.

"A few too many! That's who." He smiled at me and winked. "It's getting to be a problem. The other day Lindsey was over when the other one stopped by."

My mother nodded, looking down, a half smile on her face.

"What did you do?" I asked. My voice sounded like a squeak. But I was interested. I wanted to know what he'd done when two of his girlfriends showed up at the same time.

"Oh, I told a few little fibs. White lies." He ruffled his hand through the air, like he was mixing it up, shuffling girls in and out. "Mind you, I think they caught on."

I imagined him running up and down the stairs. Lindsey lying on the bed upstairs, under the covers, eyeliner around her eyes, her hair spread out over the pillow. Him running downstairs in his brown towelling robe to answer the door and seeing the other girl. Making an excuse, nervous, but a little bit excited.

The waiter came and filled the wineglasses. Just as he was walking away my father said, "Excuse me?" The waiter turned to him. "You filled these too high," he said, and pointed to where the wine came to in the glass.

The waiter opened his eyes wide the way a child stares and looked down at the two glasses. "You think so?"

"I know so," my father said. "You should only fill the glass halfway. First of all, it's a ton to lift," he picked up the glass by the stem, his little finger floated out. "It should have a delicate feel."

The waiter's face flushed a bright red from trying so hard, standing so straight, polishing his shoes every day before work, and now failing like this, two glasses of red wine filled too high.

"If it's white wine it's even more important to only pour it yea high." My father levelled his hand at the centre of the glass. "So it stays cold." He whispered that part, like he was letting him in on a special secret.

"Mine's fine, I don't mind how high it's filled," my mother told the waiter. She had almost finished her glass.

"Mind you, if you buy it by the glass that's a different story; then you want it filled higher. You want what you pay for. Right?" My father grinned at him, trying to make him laugh as though they were two old mates in a pub.

The waiter nodded at my father, trying to smile, but it wavered.

"You embarrassed that boy," my mother said when he had gone. "Who cares where the wine comes to?"

"If you're a waiter in a posh restaurant, you should know the proper way to pour a glass of wine," he said calmly, flatly, like nothing in the world could make this less important to him.

I took little bites of the potato on top. It was cool now, but something in my stomach felt tight. I wanted my father to be the way he was before, with his funny accents and tricks. Now we were all serious, cutting and chewing our food. My mother drank her wine quickly. The only sound was the scraping of the knives and forks against our plates.

When we were finished and the table was cleared, a man wheeled the dessert trolley over. It was a different waiter. He was older, taller, with dark black hair turning grey in places. He stood up straight and tall with his hands wrapped tightly around the handle of the trolley. He stared straight ahead and let us look. There were little white cards with the names of the cakes and puddings written on them, like place headings at a dinner party. There were round light pastries filled with whipped cream and covered in chocolate. A trifle in a glass bowl that you could see the layers through, thick and striped: the yellow of the custard, the white of the whipped cream, the sponge cake, and a sprinkle of red raspberries. On the top shelf, the cakes rose up like expensive decorated hats on silver dishes, some rounded, some flat. A purple one with crystallized petals around the edge, a chocolate cake with milk-white chocolate shavings on top, and, in crystal glasses, chocolate mousse with whipped cream on top.

"Yummy, yummy," my father said slowly, rubbing his hands together. "What would you like, my dear?" he asked, leaning towards me, smiling, as though he were offering me anything I wanted in the world.

I couldn't decide. It was too much, all brightly feathered, all perfect.

My father ordered profiteroles and three spoons. The wine bottle was finished, and the waiter asked if we wanted anything else to drink. My father shook his head.

"A Cointreau, please," my mother said to the waiter.

"You're drinking a lot," my father said, digging his spoon into one of the chocolate-covered cream puffs.

I dragged my spoon across the top, gathering the chocolate by itself and tasting it: a tiny, slow bite. That was how I ate sweets, in slow doll-size bites, so they would last.

"So what do think, Lucy? Sounds like a good idea to me if I do say so myself." He was talking about the wine bar, Dandelions. I saw the name above the door in pale yellow script. Men in tight trousers and purple shoes walking in, fancy cars outside.

"It does sound like a good idea," she said, nodding. She finished her drink and put the glass down on the table. She was talking slower now. When the waiter went by she said, "Another Cointreau, please.

"But I don't have any money to invest." Her face was still in the dark, under a shadow. I looked up to see what was covering her. The head and long neck of a deer hung from a plaque on the wall, its eyes wide open, shiny. I remembered when we studied Eskimos in school. Before they cooked their fish, they would draw their hands over its face, gently closing the fish's eyes.

"You could always take a out a second mortgage or sell and move back to London. That way I could see May more. Money makes money. It's true, it really does." He said it like he knew, like he was the god of money.

"I don't want to move back to London," she said slowly, following my eyes up to where I stared at the deer's head.

Then he looked up. "That's great-looking, majestic," he said, admiring it as though it were alive.

When the bill came, he tossed a credit card down on the table. He didn't even look at it.

Then the older waiter came back, holding the card in the palm of his hand and placing it softly on the table.

"I'm sorry, sir, but the card was denied."

"Oh," my father said, reaching into the pocket of his jacket and pulling out a thin brown card-size wallet. He took another one out and tossed it down. That's how men do it, they just toss it down.

"Thank you, Dad," I said. He was leaning back, his head against the wall, his arm reaching over, onto my mother's lap. She'd finished her drink and her eyes were closing.

"Pleasure, darling."

I was afraid of the drive home.

...

When we returned, Annabel and Patricia were in the sitting room. They sat facing each other on the sofa with their feet curled up beneath them. The television was on low, but they weren't watching it. Patricia hugged a cushion to her chest. They looked like two girls who had been up all night, talking about boys, telling each other ghost stories.

Eden was asleep on the floor, under a red tartan blanket with a fringe on the edge.

"Lucy. You'll never believe who Patricia had an affair with," Annabel said excitedly, as we walked in: my mother, my father, and I.

"Just a fling, really," Patricia said. "And I was twenty-one." She giggled.

There was a half-eaten Cadbury's Fruit and Nut bar, a teapot and two teacups, a glass of Ribena, and a packet of crisps on the table, cigarettes, an ashtray, and the December *Tatler*.

"Charlie Watts!" Annabel said, banging her hand down on her thigh like a quick clap, a tiny firework. I knew who he was; Charlie Watts was one of the Rolling Stones. In London, Annabel, Suzy, and my mother would sit cross-legged on the floor, all the Rolling Stones' records spread out in front of them, and talk about which one was the sexiest. My mother always said Bill Wyman, Annabel said Mick Jagger, and Suzy liked Keith Richards. They'd talk about them as if they were their best friends. Once Suzy flew in, out of breath, a long striped scarf around her neck. "I just bumped into Mick walking down the Kings Road!" she told us. "Mick and Keith," that's what they called them.

"Oh." My mother nodded, sitting down on the floor, taking off her high-heeled shoes.

My father sat down on the butterfly chair and began to roll a joint.

"Lucy always thought Bill was the sexiest of them all," Annabel said.

"No, I didn't, I couldn't stand him," my mother said, looking at her sharply. This is how we save ourselves, flinging the knife.

She stood up and began to walk out of the room.

"Where are you going?" Annabel asked.

"I have to pee," she said, walking slowly, her arms floating up at her sides as though she were walking on a line, trying not to fall.

"Simon, dearest," Annabel said, leaning towards him with a tight, thin smile on her face. "You didn't bring us a little something, did you?" She gestured with her finger under her nose and a little sniff. He was sitting back in the chair lighting the long joint, one gold cufflink showing.

"I might have done," he said. Puffs of smoke came out in each word. His face looked grey.

"Here." It sounded like "ear" when he said it. He handed her the joint. He stood up, pulled his shoulders back, and walked out of the room. I watched him, his walk, moving forward from the hips, his head up high, looking around.

I sat next to Annabel on the sofa, looking at the telly, at the table, chewing on my fingernail.

"Did you have a nice supper?" Patricia asked me.

I nodded.

My father came back in the room carrying a little plate, a toast plate, and set it down carefully on the table. Patricia cleared a spot, pushing things out of the way with the back of her hand. It was a dark blue plate with tiny white leaves around the edge. In the middle was a pile, a thimbleful, of white powder. Like salt, like sugar.

He hitched his trousers up before sitting down and took out a ten-pound note and a credit card. Once, in London, someone had left a note on the table. I found it in the morning, a five-pound note. I unrolled it, then I flattened it out under two heavy books.

My mother came back in, holding four wineglasses and a bottle of wine. Her hair had come undone and fell over her shoulders, the clip loose in the back.

"Why isn't Eden in his bed?" she asked Annabel.

"He fell asleep and we didn't want to wake him," Annabel said. They were passing the plate and the rolled-up note around.

My mother sat down on the chair facing the sofa. Sometimes she looked so young, not like a girl or a teenager, but just after. Like her children should still be babies.

"May, I think it's your bedtime," she said to me.

"After the adverts," I said, looking at the telly. She knew I wasn't watching, but it was Saturday night and my father was here.

"Where's Rufus? Maybe he would like a glass of wine." That was my mother; it came out in a rush. Then she looked down, fingering the edge of Eden's blanket.

"Oh, Rufus has been working so hard. He goes to the library, then comes home and does more work," Patricia said, a patch of white powder on the tip of her nose.

"You must inspire him," Annabel said, and when she looked at Patricia, it was all wonder.

"He calls me his muse," Patricia said, stretching out the words like a high song.

There was a look on my mother's face, something hard between her eyes.

"He wants to hurry up and finish so we can go back to London."

"You live in London?" my father asked, passing her the joint.

"Yes." She inhaled lightly, her lips around it like a baby kiss.

"When are you two leaving?" my mother asked.

"I'm not sure, in a day or two."

"Oh, good," my mother said, her hand holding the glass, her eyes on the wall.

Then everything stopped. The plate my father held out to Patricia froze in the air, his wrist stiff and long. It was like watching the seconds on a clock and nothing else. They looked at my mother, then away from her.

"What part of London do you live in?" my father asked, when she took the plate from him.

"South Kensington," Patricia said slowly, moving around the card on the plate, taking a long time in order to have something to do.

"Come on, May, let's go to bed," my mother said, standing up and holding out her hand to me. I didn't take it. I pushed myself up.

"You'll have to give me your address so I can invite you to the opening of my new restaurant," my father said to Patricia.

"A restaurant! I'd love to come." She jumped up a little, her hands on her knees, smiling at my father.

"Goodnight," I said, standing up, waving.

"Are you feeling all right, Lucy? You look a little pale," Annabel said, her mouth in a frown.

"I'm fine," my mother said. Then she walked out of the room.

I stood there for a minute with my hands on the back of the butterfly chair.

"What kind of food?" Annabel asked.

"I thought we'd have lots of little tasties, really delicious things: a Moroccan dish, a French dish, good old jolly old, maybe an Indian, some Tapas."

"Okay, good night," I said again, waiting for my father to give me a kiss. But he didn't; he just looked up at me and everyone said goodnight at the same time, like a birthday song.

I left quickly, as though I hadn't been waiting for anything, never expecting anything. I could hear them as I walked down the hallway to my room.

"Tapas? I absolutely love Tapas."

"So do I," Annabel said.

I knew what would happen next. They would keep passing that plate around and talk about boring things for a long time. And Eden, asleep on the floor under the red tartan blanket, wouldn't miss a thing.

Sixteen

hen I woke up the next morning I felt like I was pushing myself through water. It was Sunday. Outside, each cloud was a different grey. There was a tight feeling in my hands, and I remembered my father was here. I had to look, watching, to make my fingers open.

I walked to the kitchen to make tea with milk and honey, but before I got there I turned around and went back to my room, closing the door behind me. I didn't want him, my father, to see me like this, in my too-short nightgown and with tangled hair. I stood in front of the oval mirror on my chest of drawers and brushed my hair. The chest was made of a pale wood with tiny painted poppies on it. My grandmother gave it to me; she called it my baby furniture. We used to have a whole set, but some got lost or left behind in London. Barbara's invitation sat right in the middle; it was soon, her party.

I thought, This is how you become a teenager and then a woman, brushing your hair first thing in the morning, an invitation to a party on your desk. Pulling on your jeans and a tight sweater, looking at yourself sideways in the mirror, flattening your hand over your belly, sighing, holding it in, then looking again. Better.

Eden sat on the floor of the sitting room, the blanket wrapped around him. His thin blond hair was pushed up at the back from where he'd slept on it. I wore my jeans, my Levi's, because I knew my father liked American things. His favourite car was a Cadillac.

The cartoons were on. It was almost eight o'clock on a Sunday morning, ten days before Christmas.

I stood next to Eden, watching the cartoon. It was the one about the carousel ponies who come alive at night and talk, and the only person who knows is this one little boy.

Eden sipped a mug of Ribena through a Crazy Straw. You could watch the purple come up slowly and wind around upside down like a roller coaster; then you tasted it, the blackberry sweetness on your tongue. He must have spent the whole night here, on the floor.

"Did you sleep here all night, Eden?"

He nodded, staring at the telly.

"I went out to supper with my father last night," I said. I held my hands together in front of me. When he turned to look at me, his eyes were the same bright blue as his pyjama top and his face was round and puffy from just waking up.

"I already know that," he said to me, very slowly, and turned his face back to the telly. Eden hardly ever asked about his father; he didn't care about him. He was a boy with both hands wrapped around one candle.

It was warm in the room. The song from the cartoon played softly. Eden sipped his drink, making loud sucking and bubbling noises with the straw.

"My name comes from an old word that means bear cub," Eden said, when the advert came on.

"Who told you that?" I sat down on my knees with my feet under me. Everything from last night was still on the table except the rolled-up note; someone else had taken it.

"Rufus told me. And in Hebrew it means paradise." His voice cracked in parts. It was one of the first things he had said today.

"Last night, when I stayed here with Nanny Annabel . . ." This made him start laughing, a squeaky sound, his whole head and shoulders bopping up and down.

"Stop laughing!" I said, and flung my hand down on his knee. He looked at it, at the spot I hit, surprised. There was something sharp in the middle of my chest, like a splinter.

"Then Annabel and that other woman went to the pub to buy cigarettes, and they got me a licorice and sherbet." Each word he said was a wooden block on top of wooden blocks. "And when they were gone I stayed downstairs with Rufus and we did my Velveteen Rabbit puzzle."

"There are pieces missing," I said.

"Only three." This is how he pronounced three: fwee. "He told me what my name means in other languages too. He's going to write it all down and give it to me."

Eden said this like it was a secret, something special to be saved, a bag of jam doughnuts behind his back.

"He thinks I'm smart, he told me that." Eden really believed it. I could see it in his face, in the way he didn't answer me right away, and in the way he didn't want to know what I did last night. He was a little more sure this morning, a little more on his own.

"Actually, he thinks you're annoying."

Eden tilted his head to one side, looking at me.

"Why do you think he's leaving early? He can't finish his book because he says we are always bothering him." I told Eden this, keeping my face very still and serious, just moving my mouth so the words came out in one straight line.

"But he wanted to do the puzzle. I wasn't bothering him."

Something clear passed over his face, like a wave. His cheeks turned red.

"Well, that's what I heard." I was imitating a voice that I had heard somewhere, a thin-faced woman in a tweed suit and skin-coloured stockings, rolling a pen like a seesaw between two fingers. And it was the truth, I *had* really heard that, sitting in the hallway with my fingers wrapped around my toes in the dark. No one checked to see if I was in bed asleep, no one poked their head out of the kitchen door to make sure I wasn't listening. So Eden should be allowed to hear it too.

I stood up like I had other things to do this morning, like I didn't care. Eden looked at me, watching me, the way you watch a balloon that you let go of float up and up until you are sure you can't see it any more, until it's just the plain wide sky.

The way his bright, clear hair stuck up in places, the way his eyes drooped, made him look like something just hatched, something new. And I was ruining it, early on a Sunday morning. I ran my hand over the bottom part of my stomach, over the buttons of the jeans, and took a deep breath, sucking it in. Just like a woman, I thought. Just like a woman does.

...

I wished there were a lock on my bedroom door. I ate cereal standing up in the kitchen. This is what weekend mornings were like in London: eating cereal standing up on the morning-cold kitchen floor, waiting for my mother to wake up.

I thought of the cliff by the sheep pasture. I imagined running forward with my eyes closed and then the falling-over part. I would want to look, would need to; I couldn't just jump up and over. I wouldn't be able to pretend it was just a diving board. I kept eating, holding the bowl close to me, right under my chin. My cup of tea was on the counter beside me. Then I saw myself at the bottom on the rocks, loose and collapsed, the same way I thought Eden would look. And the woman from the jumble sale, the one who had called me a "haunting little thing" in front of Barbara Whitmore's mother, would say, "That little thing with them bad teeth what fell off the cliff."

It was nine now and my father was here, somewhere in this house, asleep in bed in one of the guest rooms. Since he'd been here, I'd looked in the mirror more than I ever had before.

The Christmas holidays started soon, so we didn't have much homework. I thought about Barbara's party and that my father was here for Christmas. Those two things, the party and my father, mixing together like the ingredients of a spell, and making everything sparkle.

I went to my bedroom and dragged the old boot box out from under my bed. In the box were used Christmas cards I'd saved so that I could cut them up and make my own ones. There were nail scissors for cutting out tiny things: the stars, the snowflakes, the red-breasted birds sitting on a snowy branch, and the holly. There were pieces of cut-up thick coloured paper (greyish blue, pinky orange, brick red) and some plain white pieces too. I filled up a glass jar of warm water to rinse the paintbrushes in. They were in the tin paint-box with the teddy bear sticker on the inside. I had three tubes of glitter: gold, silver, and a mixture with shiny green and red in it. The coloured pencils all needed sharpening. There were other things in the box too, tissue paper and ribbons, glue, a rabbit-shaped button.

My head felt heavy on my neck from bending over. The floor was sprinkled with little bits of paper, like someone had thrown a tight handful up and let it sprinkle down. I picked up the card I'd made. It was damp from the glue, and I put it on the radiator to dry. There was a row of white Christmas trees, small ones, at the bottom. On the top I wrote *Happy Christmas* in glue and covered it in silver glitter. In the middle of the card, things floated around: a butterfly, a present in a box with a bow, a candlestick.

Putting the tip of my finger in my mouth, looking down at the card drying on the radiator I thought for a minute—who I could give it to. My father would think it looked like something messy. There were other things he wanted to look at; cars and stereo equipment. I wanted to give it to Rufus; he would look at everything and know how long it had taken. Then he would save it somewhere safe, in between the pages of a book, forever, even if I never saw him again.

I went to see if my mother was awake; she never slept this late. It was quiet in the house. Everyone was still asleep except for me and Eden. They must have stayed up all night, sitting in the living room, watching it get brighter and brighter outside.

I stood in the kitchen looking at the clock. It was almost eleven. There was a sound at the door, a knocking sound. Someone was knocking at the door of our flat. I froze like a watched insect, my eyes on a corner of the floor.

I heard a man's voice, muffled, bumping through the walls, and then I heard Eden's voice. I looked out and saw Eden standing at the end of the hallway talking to Rufus.

"Hi, May," Rufus said, as I walked towards him. He was standing on the step outside the door.

"Look, May. See? Look how many different things my name means," Eden said, holding up a piece of paper with typed words on it. He still had the blanket wrapped around him, the bottom dragging on the floor.

"So?" I stood next to him, stepping on the bottom of his blanket. He moved against the wall, away from me, trying to pull the blanket, but it was stuck under my feet.

"Is Lucy here?" Rufus asked.

"Lucy?"

"Your mum."

"I'll look," I said, and ran down the hallway loudly, like a child. I wanted her to wake up. I put my hand tightly on the knob and turned it; then I pushed the door open as though it were a heavy wooden gate.

The floor of my mother's bedroom was scattered with clothes. The curtains were closed; the room was hazy. A pair of big shoes were by the door, my father's suede shoes. My mother lay on her side at the edge of the bed with her hands tucked underneath the pillow. My father lay next to her, on his back, his arms slack at his sides. A dark patch of hair on his chest rose and fell with each loud breath he took. They were both asleep. The sheets and pale yellow blanket fell down my mother's back, the bones in her shoulders stuck out like butterfly wings.

I stepped backward out of the room, pulling the door quietly closed. I stared at the door, at the thin lines in the paint. I had never seen my mother and father in the same bed before. When I walked down the hall the walls seemed nearer.

"They're sleeping," I said to Rufus. He looked at me for a minute but didn't say anything.

"My mum and dad are still asleep, in bed." My voice sounded loud.

Then he knew that they were both asleep, together: Lucy and Simon, my mother and father, in one bed.

"Oh." His eyes went flat and he looked away from me. "Okay. I'll just come back later." He was talking fast, about to turn and walk down the stairs.

"Is that man in my mum's room?" Eden asked in a whisper.

"My father," I said. Eden leaned his back against the wall and looked up at the ceiling.

"Is she happy? I mean, that he's here?" Rufus asked softly. His face looked pale. This question must have been in his head since last night when Patricia said it. I didn't know. It was something I never thought about, my mother's happiness.

"You must be glad he's here." Then I had to hold my breath; I felt it close to my eyes. I waited, and he looked at Eden, who was standing against the wall, his hands behind his back, as small as he could be.

I wanted to tell Rufus everything: the way my mother asked about him, how she kept the note he had given her in a painted box. I wanted him to know the truth. His face looked so clean and wide, a field without hunters.

"She thinks you were only pretending to be her friend." My voice shook when I said it.

"What?" I saw his hand hold the banister tight.

Then I couldn't say anything else. My throat hurt inside, but he kept looking at me, waiting.

"Why does she think that?"

It's hard to tell anyone the whole truth, to give it all away. I still wasn't sure with him. You have to be careful; people have hidden drawers and corners, and everyone has pieces of glass inside.

"May, please tell her I want to talk to her when she wakes up." It sounded serious, like echoes down a hospital wall.

I nodded, but I had to look up at the ceiling because my eyes felt wet.

The day was different now. It was still morning, but it felt as though it were late at night when you can't sleep. I went to my room and made another Christmas card.

...

"Mum?" It was later now, darker; outside, the clouds looked like they were just a reach away. My mother, Eden, and I were cooking in the kitchen. Annabel and my father were still asleep.

"Look." I held up the first card I'd made. The second one was still drying on the radiator.

"It's beautiful," my mother said. She put her hand on the top of my head and ran it over my hair and the top of my back.

"What time did you go to bed?" There was something in her face and in her wrist today, like the white from her bones was shining through her skin.

"I don't know, before the rest of them." I imagined Annabel, Patricia and my father in the sitting room, it turning light outside, my father staring at Patricia's legs, then crawling into bed with my mother. It was already noon. My father was still asleep. He could never be a mother.

My mother crinkled rosemary and salt over the chicken. Eden was at the table, breaking the ends off the string beans. There was a whole sieve full next to him, still wet as if they had been rained on. She was wearing her old jeans with a big sweater and her moccasin slippers. Her hair was bunched up on the top of her head. The radio played Christmas songs, and Eden's head went bobbing from side to side in time with them.

"How much longer is May's father going to stay?" Eden asked, twisting around in the chair, a green bean clasped in his hand. I didn't say anything. I didn't care what Eden thought about him, he seemed so small, a loose button hanging off the cuff of a jacket.

"I'm not sure," my mother said, opening the oven with a knitted cloth. A patch of warm air blew against my stomach.

"He's staying for Christmas," I said to Eden. I was picking out potatoes from a big basket of them, dirt-covered and brown. "Should I scrub them in the sink?" I piled the potatoes up in my T-shirt and carried them to the sink.

Outside, the bare branches of the tree reached up and up to the sky; that's what they do. I stood on the footstool by the sink and let the water run, cold and clean. I pretended it was a swimming pool for the potatoes and scrubbed them with the vegetable brush. It was warm in the kitchen. With the carols playing on the radio, it felt like the best place in the world to be right then.

I heard a door close behind me and my shoulders tightened. "What was that sound?"

"I just closed the door so we wouldn't wake Simon," my mother said. I could tell she didn't want him to wake up. I felt my shoulders drop down, loosen. I turned back to the sink, to the cold water. Something happened to me when my father was around, I never knew what to do with my hands. I didn't want him to see me right then, with mud spots on my wrist.

Someone knocked on the kitchen door. It sounded strange, as if this door would open to the grass and trees outside. I pretended this one room was our whole house, a safe feeling.

My mother opened the door, wiping her hand down the top of her jeans. Rufus stood there, his eyes wide the way they went whenever he first saw her.

"Lucy," he said. It flew up like a swing.

"Hello." My mother clutched a dishcloth in her hand.

"Hi, Rufus." Eden waved from his seat, his small pile of green beans in a neat row next to him.

My mother kept her eyes level, like they were stuck on one place on the wall behind him.

"How are you?" he asked.

She took a step back, away from him, and said, "I'm fine, thanks. How are you?" It was tight, the sound of her voice, like my grandmother's.

"All right." It was small, under his foot, the way he said it.

There was an advertisement on the radio, and neither of them spoke. My mother opened a drawer, looking for something, then closed it again.

"I feel like I haven't seen you in a long time," Rufus said.

She didn't answer.

"I finished the translation," he said excitedly.

"That's great, Rufus, you must be pleased." The tone of her voice was an ironed sheet.

He nodded, lifting his shoulders up and dropping them down. The way he moved wasn't like my father, who was always leaning back slowly, bringing a cigarette to his mouth.

"I wanted to see—" Rufus began saying, slowly.

"Did you want to pay your bill?" my mother asked, jumping in quickly, a bunny hop.

"What?" He looked startled and made a sound like a sigh, like he was dropping something. "Lucy?"

"Yes?"

"I was wondering if you wanted to take a walk with me?"

"A walk? I'm in the middle of cooking lunch," she said, like it was a ridiculous idea.

"What about later? Should I come back later?" He looked as though he were walking over something that might suddenly break underneath him. Taking one careful step at a time, stopping and waiting, before he took the next step. My mother just watched him, struggling across the ice, not even reaching out her arm to help him.

She put the top on the honey jar, picked up a spoon, and dropped it in the sink with the potatoes and water. She didn't know what she was doing; she was just doing anything, while he stood holding on tightly to the back of a chair.

Finally she stopped moving around and stood still, looking straight at him. I thought, Now she'll stop and tell him everything; she'll say, *Tell me the truth, Rufus, because this is what I heard.* But instead she said flatly, as though she were setting a table, "Rufus, I don't know what impression I gave you, but I was just trying to be polite. I was being friendly."

She could hold her jug of silence to the end, without spilling a single drop. Who was he anyway? She would tell herself until it became the truth: He was just a man who wanted the quietest rooms. Other men had stayed in those rooms, and others would again.

"That bed is a bloody rock," my father said loudly, as he walked into the kitchen, stretching his arms up. He was wearing my mother's green and pink Japanese robe. It was too short for him in the arms.

"Make me a cuppa tea, darling," he said to my mother, patting her on the bum.

Rufus looked away quickly, the way you lift your finger off something hot. My mother stood frozen. I thought, She's too embarrassed to move.

"Hello, I'm Simon," my father said, introducing himself to Rufus.

"This is Rufus, he's a guest here," my mother said, but didn't look at them.

"Did anyone phone me?" my father asked, as he looked out of the window. "I'm expecting a very important call."

"Rufus?" That was Eden, saying his name like it was a question. "Was I bothering you last night? When we did the puzzle?" He was rocking backwards and forwards on his feet.

"No." Rufus swallowed as he spoke. In his face, around his eyes and mouth, a thin crack started.

"Okay. I was just wondering," Eden said, and went back to his chair at the table.

"Put a piece of toast in for me, babes," my father said to me. I pulled out the plug at the bottom of the sink; it made a gurgling sound. When I looked back, Rufus was gone.

I picked up the phone to call Jolene.

"I'm expecting a very important call," my father said again. I put the phone down.

"Rufus? What a horrible name, poor geezer. What did he want?"

"To pay the bill." She had her arms crossed in front of her and her voice sounded dry. She held her mouth closed tight.

"He probably thought he could sweet-talk you out of it."

My mother dropped a teabag in the pot. "Probably."

She buttered the toast, spread marmalade over it, then put it on a plate in front of my father, who sat smoking a cigarette.

"Look at that." He pointed to the piece of toast. "Plop, plop! That's not how you spread jam, it doesn't even go to the corners. You just plopped it right down in the middle. It's no wonder you haven't found a man yet." He was looking over at me, making a funny face. "Plop, plop!" he said again to me, so that I would laugh, and I did, from my throat, like a cheap present.

Seventeen

We sang Christmas carols next day at the morning assembly. This was my favourite part of school, like the way it used to be, before we had lessons, when it was all painting and sitting cross-legged on the floor having stories read to us.

The headmistress read us poems about wintertime and frost in her high-tea voice. I could feel the bones in my back against the wooden pew. Jolene sat in the row in front of me. I pulled lightly on a piece of her hair, but she stared straight ahead. Then I poked her between the shoulders.

"Stop it!" she said, turning around as though she was trying to swat something.

I put my hands together on my lap and held them there until assembly was over.

...

I followed Jolene outside to the school yard. She hurried ahead, as though she were trying to catch up with someone in front of her.

"Jolene! Wait." I touched the sleeve of her coat near the elbow. It was a damp day. A gentle wind rose up, like a small wave, and blew against us, the softest splash.

"Sorry—that I didn't come Christmas shopping with you on Saturday—" I began to say. She was looking over her shoulder into the playground. It was break and everyone was running towards the middle.

"It doesn't matter," Jolene said. She held her lips tightly together and looked away from me. Neither of us spoke. We were standing by the side steps against the wall where the teachers come out between classes and sit on the bench with a cup of tea and a cigarette.

"My dad came from London," I said, brightening my voice, throwing it up like confetti. "That's why. I just forgot, I'm sorry, Jolene." She twisted the wooden button on her coat. In the winter we all wore navy duffel coats with pointy hoods.

"Your dad came?" She looked up at me.

"He has a Porsche. It's red. We can go for a ride in it." When you don't have anything to say about someone, you have to talk about their things.

She put her hand over her mouth; her eyes opened wide. "Oh, my God!" she said.

"What?"

"Nothing," she said, shaking her head. She was trying not to laugh, but her face was turning red.

"What?" My fingers and hands turned suddenly cold.

"A man in a red Porsche stopped at my dad's pub for a beer and tried to pay for it with a Diners Club card." She began to giggle from her stomach, her chest shaking up and down.

"So?" I didn't see what was so funny about that. I stared at her; she looked like something you could pop right then.

"When he left, one of the men at the bar said, 'Who does he think he is, all dressed up like that? The Ponce of Monte Carlo?' And everyone in the pub started laughing."

I pictured the men in the pub, dressed in tweed jackets and woollen sweaters, their hands wrapped around wide glasses of beer.

They would turn their heads, slightly and slowly, staring out of the corners of their eyes. My father, letting the door fall shut behind him as he strolled in, smoothing a hand over his hair, looking around, thinking he looked great.

This is how the men at the bar would start laughing: like tiny white lights being lit one after another.

In the middle of the school yard the younger girls were skipping—the flat tapping of their shoes, the rope hitting the ground—and they were singing:

> "My mother told me I never should
> Play with the gypsies in the wood.
> If I did, she would say,
> Naughty little girl to run away."

I watched them standing in a row. I was looking for a younger me. I thought life was like that, all the same story.

A girl hung upside down on the monkey bars, her hair falling down like water. Across the school yard, Barbara, Courtney and Polly were sitting by the gates. A few other girls stood around them, as though they were a bright light.

"Barbara invited me to her birthday party," I said. My stomach felt full of cold water that tasted of metal.

Jolene looked at me, narrowing her eyes. "Why would she invite you?"

"Because we're friends." This is how things end: Something turns nut-hard in your chest.

"Right." She clicked her tongue.

Jolene and I looked over at them. The others had gone now, and the three girls sat on the painted green bench with their heads and hands held close together as though they were untangling knots in a thin gold chain.

"Why don't you go over there?" Jolene said.

I was waiting for the party. That's when I thought we would become friends: late at night, in our pyjamas, sitting close together, telling each other our secrets. Then we'd sneak to the kitchen, tiptoeing past her parents' bedroom, for a big bowl of crisps and sweets and cups of fizzy lemonade. Then we'd sneak back upstairs, holding our breath, trying to be quiet, then burst into giggles. Something would come out of me that night, at the party, the golden bird in my chest. Then I would really be me, and the three of them would become the four of us.

Jolene and I stood facing each other. I thought everyone in the schoolyard could hear us, that they would know, but when I looked around they were busy in groups and playing games. No one was watching us.

"Go on, then," Jolene said to me.

I turned, taking slow steps towards them. I didn't want to leave her. It is safer, even in a fight, to stay with the person you know. Where was the lunch bell? *Ring, ring,* I said in my head like a prayer.

A red ball rolled past my feet and two younger girls ran by holding hands, their hair soft as petals behind them. They made a strange sound, something between a laugh and a scream. It ends at some age, that sound; it just doesn't come out of your mouth any more.

Barbara, Courtney, and Polly now stood huddled against the wall, their backs to the schoolyard.

"Hello." I waved, but they didn't hear me. "Hi." I could hear my heart, the way it sounds underwater.

Courtney turned with a jump. "Oh," she said, when she saw me. "I thought you were one of the teachers." She held her cigarette behind her back.

"May, come here." Barbara waved me towards them. "Stand in front of us and tell us if you see Miss Higgins coming." I knew

Jolene was watching. I hummed and skipped from side to side, so she would think I was having fun.

The bell rang, they threw their cigarettes on the ground, rubbing them out with the toes of their shoes. We walked across the school yard together, the four of us.

Later, when I passed Jolene in the hall, I said, "See." It came out the corner of my mouth, a smirk.

...

Something fast was inside of me as I walked home. I swung my arms sharply at my side, like a soldier. Everything in my head was pieces of what I had said to Jolene and what she had said to me. We'd had fights before but this was different, the way we had both turned so quickly with the tips of our spears pointing at each other's throats.

I thought, I have to get the photo of Jet. I was scared that Jolene would tell them I didn't know him, but the photo would be proof.

I called Patricia's name as I walked down the stone steps and along the passage that led to her room. I knew what people looked like when they felt like me. I'd seen them on the streets in London, hunched over and walking fast, the way you look when too many things are in your way.

Cold air fell off the walls like pieces of ice. Someone had turned the heat off. I called Patricia's name, but there was no answer. Her door was slightly open, a slant of afternoon light fell across the floor in front of me. I looked inside. The sheets had been stripped, the mattress and pillows left out to air. The chair was empty, no clothes piled on it. The chest of drawers was empty. In some places there was still the smell of her.

I walked across the hall to Rufus's room. The desktop was clear; his typewriter and pile of books were gone. There was only the furniture and the low humming sound of an empty room left behind. The heat had been turned off and I could nearly see my breath in the air.

...

"The minute I get back to London I'm going to sign up for those calisthenics classes." I could hear Annabel's voice coming from the kitchen. "They have this amazing teacher from America. She swears I can lose half a stone on the Astronaut Diet in three days, just in time for my holiday in the South of France—"

When I walked into the kitchen, Annabel put her hand over something, covering it. My father was standing by the phone, his hands in his pockets, looking out of the window.

"Hello, madame," she said to me. Her eyes were like jewels that pointed and sparkled at each end. A rolled-up pound note lay on top of a record cover.

"Did you have a nice day at school?" my father asked. It was the first time he'd asked me about school since he'd been here.

"Yup. I hung out with my friend Barbara." I thought everyone would know, just by her name.

"Hung out? Don't they give you any work there?" he said.

"It's almost Christmas holidays. . . ."

He picked up the phone and began dialling a number from a small piece of paper in his hand.

"Oh, Patricia asked me to give this to you before she left," Annabel said, handing me an envelope.

Inside was a photograph of Jet. His hair fell around his face, half covering his eyes. He was standing in front of what looked like a kitchen sink, a guitar hanging across his bare chest. So it was true, I thought, the one true thing about her.

"Engaged." My father put the phone down.

"Dad?" He was looking in his pockets for a cigarette. "Dad?" I wanted to ask him something, but he didn't hear me.

"Simon!" Annabel said it quick and loud, like a spoon hitting the floor.

"What?" He looked up, surprised.

"Do you think . . . can you drive me to Barbara's party the day after tomorrow?" I held my hands tightly together in two fists at my side.

"Yeah, sure, babes," he said, looking at me.

The phone rang. He picked it up slowly, like he was pulling it out of the water, holding it in the air, letting it drip.

"Hello," he said; it sounded like *'ello*. "Fred? How are you, man?" He laughed quietly, resting his hand on his hip. "Not bad, not too bad. . . . Yeah. . . . Quite nice, a bit bleak, you know what it's like, a little village and whatnot. . . . Any news about the business?"

Annabel flipped through her magazine, one ear tilted up. Under the table I saw Eden's brown buckle shoes and satchel.

"Mitch Mitchell. . . . That sounds great, man. . . . Yeah, yeah." He paced the length of the phone cord. "All righty, mate, all right. . . . Sounds good, man, I'll be there."

When he put the phone down, he took a deep breath and stared out of the window.

"What was all that about Mitch Mitchell?" Annabel asked.

"He's interested in becoming an investor. He's having a Christmas party. We've been invited to—"

"Who's Mitch Mitchell?"

"Who's Mitch Mitchell?" Annabel said, throwing her head back as if she couldn't believe it. "He was the drummer for Jimi Hendrix, darling."

"If we get Mitch and Keith to invest we'll be all set," he said, jumping into a dance move, spinning around on one foot, tucking his arms under his elbows, and flapping them like a chicken. "It's gonna be the funkiest place in London."

"Where's Eden?" I asked.

They both stopped and looked at each other, their eyebrows lifting. Annabel bent over, peeking under the table.

"May, be an angel, run off and find your brother. Quick! Off you go." She shooed the air with the top of her hand.

I could hear her talking as I walked down the hall.

"I'm coming to the party, Simon. You have to take me. Promise, just promise me this one thing." I imagined her standing next to him, grabbing his arm tightly, hopping up and down on her toes.

I walked slowly down the hallway, my hands tightly together. When I tried to open them, uncurling my fingers slowly, like something that blooms, there was something wet in my palms. I walked underneath a lamp, holding my hands out in front of me. It was blood. There were cuts, halfmoon-shaped, from where my fingernails had dug into the skin. That's what you get, I thought. That's what you get from holding on too tightly.

It was dark in my mother's room, not a night dark but the hazy blue that comes through closed curtains. My mother was lying in bed, under the covers, asleep on her side. Eden lay across the foot of the bed in his school uniform. One of his arms stretched over his head and one of his legs bent up to his chest. As though he were stepping up, reaching for something. Climbing, reaching, even while you sleep. Even while you sleep.

Eighteen

On the way to Barbara's party, we got caught behind a herd of cows that were being led to the farm for milking.

"I don't believe it," my father said, leaning his head back on the car seat, groaning. We were on Tilden Lane. Barbara's house was a few streets away.

I held the envelope with the photo of Jet on my lap; my overnight bag was on the floor next to my feet. I was wearing my white shirt with a frilly collar, my denim miniskirt, navy lace tights, and new black patent leather buttonhook shoes. There was lipstick on my lips that I had borrowed from Annabel. "Heart-shaped lips are in," she had told me. First she went around them with a lip pencil and then painted them a mauve colour. Now my lips felt too big, stinging.

My father switched on the radio. It was the news. The weatherman's voice came through, steady and serious. "Cold front with high winds, sleet and snow probable." In front of us the cows moved, side to side, with a slow sway like the back of a woman's skirt.

"Christ, I don't want to get snowed into this place," my father said to me. I nodded and looked up, out of the car window, at the sky. It was a darkening blue and not too cold, mild like plain water. The trees were still. It didn't seem like there would be bad weather.

"Come on!" my father shouted to the back of the cows. "We'll be here all night!" Nothing changed; the cows didn't care. A farmer walked up the road, leading them. I only saw the back of him, in knee-length Wellingtons and a brown jacket, his hand resting on the back of one of the cows, walking along slowly next to them, just like the cows. He would laugh if he saw us, sitting in the bright- red fast car, stuck, behind his herd. I was hoping my father wouldn't beep the horn.

"So, is this girl your best mate?"

I nodded my head. When you start lying to people, you know it's over, because you don't care anymore; you'll never know them well enough to let them find out the truth.

I felt him looking at me, at my lap, near my shoulders, the side of my face, my hair. I kept my face turned, looking out of the window at the cows, watching the sky get darker bit by bit. I squeezed my hands and toes together. The car seemed small, tight.

"You look nice tonight, darling. That outfit suits you," he said.

"Thanks." I put my hand on the window knob and rolled down the window a crack. Cool air blew in, brushing the top of my head.

"Smelly," my father said loudly, sounding it out. "Smel-ly." He held his nose like a child. I rolled the window back up. It was the cows and horses and mud and cool air, the smell of a farm.

"Do you have a little boyfriend there?" he asked.

"No, it's an all-girls overnight."

"All girls?" he said, as though he hadn't heard me.

I nodded. He was looking at me in a strange way, as though I were upside down.

"Then what'd you get all dolled up for?"

I felt my face turn warm, my cheeks. And the lipstick on my lips felt like a badge.

"Where's her house?" He seemed impatient, leaning his head back against the seat, turning the knob on the radio, but it was all news; it was that time of day.

"Over there." I pointed past the cows with my finger, but I wasn't sure. I had never been to Barbara's house before.

A man's voice came over the radio. It was the local police news. "Mr and Mrs Derby of Lord Lane have reported that their missing garden gnome was returned sometime late last night. They did not catch sight of the person, but nevertheless they are thankful to have him back."

"Thank God," my father said, letting out a loud sigh of relief. "I'll be able to sleep tonight."

I laughed, making my shoulders shake, but it sounded like little scratches.

"Can't you walk from here? We'll be here all night if we have to wait for these slowpokes," he said, and flung his arm out at the cows.

"Okay." I opened the car door and stepped out onto the road.

"Have a good time, babes," my father said, when I reached in to pick up my overnight bag.

"Thanks," I pushed the door behind me. It didn't close all the way, but I turned and walked away. He would have to lean over and close it properly himself, from the inside. That was something that would annoy him, I knew.

I held my hands together on the bag in front of me so I wouldn't turn around to wave goodbye, and I walked straight ahead on the stone road. I heard my father turn his car around. The engine roared. I thought, Maybe the wheels are stuck in the mud, but I didn't look back.

There were thatched cottages and red brick houses just a short walk away from each other. I felt the stones through the bottom of my shoes. Here the sea couldn't steal your voice; you could stand in your doorway and shout hello to the house next door, and they would hear you and wave back. Neighbours, they had neighbours on this street. Inside the windows in the houses there were tinsel and fairy lights. "Christmas is coming," I said to myself. "Christmas is coming." I stopped for a moment. The sky moved dark white away from me. You couldn't see the stars yet, but the lights inside the houses shone like gold coins. I thought, This is where they live, those girls: on this street and other streets like it.

I couldn't see the numbers of the houses on the doors. It wasn't like London, where the numbers went up and up. Here some of the houses had names. I ran to someone's house and looked up at the door, trying to see a number, but I felt like I was stealing something and ran away quickly.

I was late for the party and soon it would be completely dark. I ran on the side of the road, next to the cows, to the farmer. I felt the grass and earth soft beneath me, and something splattered against my heel. Mud, I thought, it's just mud. I didn't want to be lost, even here on this street, I didn't want to be lost.

I wiped the lipstick off with the back of my hand as I ran, and when I was right behind the farmer I said, "Excuse me?" He was looking up at something in the sky. "Do you know which house is the Whitmores'?" He pointed straight ahead. I saw it, the balloons tied to the front door. As I ran ahead I heard him yell, "Mind the ditch!" I looked down. Right to the side of me the road went down suddenly.

Mrs Whitmore answered the door, pulling it open, looking down at me. "May?" she said. I nodded. She was older than my mother. Her hair was a greyish-blond folded in neatly to her chin and her eyes two blue drops that had fallen.

"You're the last one here. We were getting worried." She leaned forward, put her arm on the top of my back, and led me inside. We stood in a small room with peach-coloured walls. There was a small wooden table with a lamp and a silver bowl full of sweets on it. "I'll hang your coat here," she said, and her fingers brushed over the tops of mine. "Cold hands," she said, taking them between hers.

"The girls are in the front room." She walked ahead of me, in her pale yellow cardigan and grey pleated skirt. She wore skin-coloured stockings with brown pumps. We walked through different rooms. In one, a man sat reading the paper. He stood up as we walked past, and Mrs Whitmore introduced me. It was Barbara's father. He was shorter than his wife, with thick grey hair and wide shoulders. He shook my hand tightly. Braces held his trousers up over a round belly. He worked at the bank.

We walked through a dining room with a long wooden table and red-cushioned chairs lined up against the walls. I could hear the girls' voices, each a gold ring thrown through the wall.

Mrs Whitmore opened the door of a long room with Victorian furniture. The girls were sitting on the floor on a white lace cloth, having a picnic. There was a fireplace, and the windows overlooked a tidy garden.

"May!" Barbara shouted, as I walked in. She sat at the head. Her hair was curled at the bottom, and she wore a candy-floss-coloured dress with ruffled sleeves. Everyone was wearing paper party hats; some had feathers in them and others said HAPPY BIRTH-DAY in silver glitter.

"Hurry! Sit in your spot; we were just about to pull the crackers!" Barbara pointed to an empty place at the other end, next to two girls from our form, Emma and Pauline. They were best friends. They looked at each other and then moved closer together, making a spot for me at the end.

A pile of brightly wrapped presents with ribbons and bows lay next to the sofa. I held on to my envelope; it would get lost over there with those boxes. Mrs Whitmore stood by the fireplace, looking at us. Two girls I had never seen before sat across from me.

They looked alike; their eyes pointed up at the sides like the tips of wings, and they both had straight dark brown hair pulled tightly off their faces. They sat up perfectly straight.

"These are my cousins, Charlotte and Clare. They can't spend the night; they have ballet tomorrow," Barbara said. One of them leaned forward, her whole body a dip and glide as she picked up one single crisp from the bowl. They didn't move like the rest of us. They seemed as though they were from another country.

"Everyone cross your arms," Maisie yelled, blowing her fringe away from her eyes. She was the field hockey goalie. We crossed our arms in front of us, taking the ends of each other's crackers.

"Go!" Maisie shouted. She was the loudest girl in our class. We pulled; there were popping sounds and sparks and the smell of gunpowder in the air. Charms and tissue-paper crowns fell onto our laps. Mine was a miniature parachute diver with a plastic parachute.

"Look!" Emma, the girl next to me, said. She held up a silver bracelet. Everyone was quiet, looking.

"It's not real?" Courtney said.

"It is, it's marked." Emma pulled it closer to her, reading a tiny silver tag on it, her brown hair falling in ringlets around her face.

Mrs Whitmore walked into the room, carrying a silver tray layered with tea sandwiches. "Cucumber, egg and mayonnaise, butter and cheese, ham and cheese." She bent down on her knees, lowering the silver tray to the floor.

"Thank you, Mummy," Barbara said. Mrs Whitmore smiled at her softly, tilting her head to the side. Then she brought in another tray of teapots, three different ones, two painted with flowers and one in the shape of a swan. The plates were white and pink paper, but we each had our own china teacup and saucer, white with green and gold flowers around the rim.

Mrs Whitmore made a soft groaning sound when she stood up, placing her hand low on her back.

"What shivers and shakes at the bottom of the ocean?" Polly asked, reading a piece of white paper.

Everyone closed their mouths, thinking. Mrs Whitmore stood at the door with her hand on the knob, waiting to hear the answer.

"Well, go on, tell us," Courtney shouted. She wore a black dress with a V shape down the back; you could see her bare skin.

"A nervous wreck!" Polly said. Mrs Whitmore shook her head, laughing.

Outside it looked dark through the windows, but inside the room it was warm from the fire. We passed around the heavy tea-pots; our hands moved over the silver sandwich tray. There were other things in front of us: fizzy drinks, coloured paper cups, a bowl of Smarties. When I looked down I saw the dried mud on the heel of my shoe and wrapped my fingers around it.

The door opened, and an older girl and boy walked in wearing ponchos, their cheeks still red from being outside. The girl was Sara, Barbara's older sister.

"Why are you all sitting on the floor?" Sara asked. She had long straight blond hair with a centre parting.

"We're having a picnic," Barbara told her. Sara kissed Barbara on the top of the head and said, "Happy birthday."

"This is my sister, Sara. She's seventeen."

"This is Oliver," Sara said, putting her arm around him.

His dark brown hair was parted on the side and pushed back behind his ears, chin length. He had a long nose and pale skin; his lips were a dark red.

"He's my boyfriend," Sara said. "Oliver's at university. He's just home for Christmas."

Oliver put his hands in his trouser pockets. Sara had gone to our school, but now she was getting her A levels.

"Gosh," we all said.

"I like your beads," Polly said to Sara.

"Thanks," she said, and walked out of the room, taking Oliver by the hand.

When they were gone, Barbara leaned forward and said in a loud whisper, "They've had sex."

"They have?" we said and covered our mouths with our hands. "Gosh," we all said again, slowly, as though we were imagining it.

"Raise your hand if you've done it," Courtney said.

We all looked at one another, but none of us raised our hands. Above us, the chandelier hung down like an umbrella of lights.

"How far have you gone?" Courtney asked Maisie.

"If my mum walks in, pretend to be talking about something else, like a book or a horse," Barbara whispered to us.

We nodded and moved in towards each other, closer together. Clare counted out five Hula-Hoop crisps and put them on her fingers like rings.

"You start," Courtney said to Maisie.

"French-kissing and feeling there." She pointed to her breasts. "And also there," she said, pointing her finger at her lap.

"Under or over clothes?"

"Under," Maisie said, then grabbed a handful of Smarties.

"What did you do to him?" Pauline asked, moving around, sitting on her heels. Polly pushed her plate and teacup forward and sat in closer.

"I touched his willy, over his trousers." Everyone giggled and made a face when she said that word, "willy".

"Next." It was Charlotte's turn, one of the ballerinas. She shook her head, her face a little pink. Then it was Clare's turn, the other ballerina. She said, "French-kissed." By the way she looked down, fingering the edge of her dress, I knew she was lying.

"Your turn, May. What have you done?" Courtney asked.

"The same as her," I said, pointing to Clare.

"With who?" Maisie asked me, leaning forward. There was something about the way she moved, walking towards things as though she might drive right through them, that made me want to stay far away from her.

"This boy in London over the summer." My face was turning red but not because I had lied; it was from something else. I kept wondering, When will we start talking about something more? Something we would have to pull out of ourselves, that would make us all the same. I wanted some kind of magic and wings, the conversation people have right before they fall in love. It was the thing I thought my father would tell me on the rocks. Upstairs, later, sitting huddled together, telling secrets—that's when it will happen, I thought.

Suddenly, the lights went out. Mrs and Mr Whitmore walked in, carrying the birthday cake. Sara and Oliver followed them, singing "Happy Birthday". Mr Whitmore bent down, almost dropping the cake, and placed it in front of Barbara. She sat up straight and took a deep breath.

"Make a wish!" her mother called out to her as she cut the first slice. There were marzipan flowers on the cake and marzipan mice. It all seemed so young. After the cake, Barbara opened the presents—records and a rainbow poster, a new denim jacket, a gold heart on a chain—tearing at the paper and bows, throwing them to the side. When she opened the picture of Jet she kissed it and hugged it to her chest, falling backward in a pretend faint.

Barbara put on a new Olivia Newton-John record. Sara showed us all the new moves, how to shimmy our shoulders and shake our hips really quickly. She tried to teach us how to spin around and flip our hair at the same time, but it flew into our mouths and we bumped into each other. Oliver sat on the sofa, tapping his foot and eating the leftover sandwiches.

"Let's do the Bus Stop!" Sara yelled excitedly. She kicked off her clogs, pulled Oliver off the sofa, and told us to line up. "Follow me!" she shouted over the music. We were in a row behind her. She had her back to us, and then she started moving her hips. "Shuffle to the side . . . lift your leg and shuffle the other way. Clap your hands and spin!"

Mr and Mrs Whitmore stood by the wall, watching, and Sara shouted, "Dad, come on!" You could tell he wanted to because he had been singing along. Mrs Whitmore blushed as she watched her husband walk over, swinging his hips.

The song was like a celebration, with all the claps and "oohs." With Sara, we were the same, all younger girls following her. The music was loud and we were hot from dancing and laughing. Every time Sara said shuffle, her father couldn't move his feet fast enough, and instead he'd shake his bum around. It was podgy and square in his beige trousers, and every time we looked at it we burst, nearly falling down. Our stomachs hurt, but we couldn't stop; everything was funny, and we collapsed on the floor, tears streaming down our bright-red faces. It's like when you get tickled so much that all someone has to do is wiggle their fingers in the air and you feel it.

Later, we went up to Barbara's bedroom. The ballerinas had been driven home, and Sara and Oliver had gone out to a party. Maisie's mother was coming to collect her, because she wasn't allowed to spend the night. She stood square and cross-armed in the hall waiting for her.

On the way upstairs, Courtney said, "Her mum won't let her stay because she wets the bed." When we passed Barbara's parents' room she poked her head in to say goodnight. They were lying in bed in their nightclothes eating a piece of cake. "Thank you for such a fun party. We're tired from all the dancing," Barbara said.

Barbara's bedroom looked as though it belonged to a child. There was a miniature armchair with a footstool, and on the shelves were rows of dolls in ball gowns with their hair still perfect. Rosebud wallpaper covered the walls, only now it was hidden in places by posters of rock stars.

Polly sat down in the small armchair, stretching her legs out in front of her. "When are they coming?" she asked.

"We have to phone them," Barbara said, leaning against the wall. She looked like a little girl in her pink dress, against the bright wallpaper, on her birthday.

"Phone who?" I asked, but Barbara wasn't listening.

I sat down on the bed next to Emma and Pauline.

Barbara picked up the phone and dragged it into the bathroom. "Court, Polly, come on," she said to them.

I moved my hands over the eiderdown; everything had flowers on it with long squiggly stems wrapping around each other. Pinned to the wall, above the bed, were photographs of Barbara, Courtney and Polly: at the beach, posing outside a shop on a city street.

Barbara came running out of the bathroom half undressed. "We have to make the beds up," she said, out of breath, as she pulled blankets and eiderdowns from the closet.

"Grab our bags," Polly and Courtney yelled from the bathroom, and Barbara rushed back in, one bag in each arm.

Emma and Pauline walked over to the pile of blankets and began folding them the long way and laying them out like sleeping bags.

"Who's coming?" I asked them.

The two of them looked at me across the room but didn't say anything for a moment. Then Pauline said, "Their boyfriends." Something about her mouth scared me; it was like touching barbed wire.

"Who? What boys?" I asked. My voice shook a little. I could hear sounds coming from the bathroom: water running, a hair dryer, the three of them talking very fast at the same time.

"Older boys, from Shepperton." Shepperton was a bigger town a few miles away.

Finally, the bathroom door opened and the three girls walked out, smelling of perfume. Polly wore a fringed suede waistcoat, tight dark blue jeans, and high-heeled shoes. Courtney had turned her black dress around, so now the V came down the front. Her hair was in a high twist and Barbara's gold heart choker was around her neck. When she moved in a certain way, you could see her small chest, her nipples.

"May?" Barbara said to me, and something in my chest lifted.

"Yes?" She stood in front of me in a red leotard.

"Can I borrow your skirt? Please." She pointed to the one I was wearing, my denim miniskirt. I unbuttoned the top button, pulled it down over my thighs, and handed it to her. I thought there was something wrong with her eyes, but it was just blue eye shadow.

"Thanks," she said, and kissed me on the cheek. I stood in my shirt and tights; then I remembered that there was a hole in the bottom of them and put my hand over it. I looked behind me but no one had noticed; they were all looking in the mirror.

Outside I heard a sound. I thought it was the wind, howling around the house.

"You might be cold," I said to Barbara, as she fastened her cork sandals. She wasn't wearing tights.

"I think you look really good, Barbara," Pauline told her, and Emma nodded in agreement. They were sitting next to each other on the bed.

I heard the sound again and walked over to the window, but Polly was dancing in front of it, looking at her reflection, the fringe of her waistcoat twirling up as she spun around. I went to the window at the other end of the room. Outside, the trees stood still. There was no wind.

"What time is it?" Courtney asked, picking up the Snoopy alarm clock on the desk.

"If my mother knocks, turn off all the lights and pretend you're asleep," Barbara told us.

"Okay," Pauline said, but she sounded worried. "Do you think she'll come up?"

Then I heard that sound again, coming through their voices: a long moan.

"What's that noise?" I asked, standing very still.

"Is it them? Was it a car horn?" Courtney asked, running to the window. Polly flipped her hair back.

"Is it them?" Barbara asked, standing behind her, their voices high and shaky.

Courtney shook her head. "No one's there."

"I'm dying for a fag," Polly said, flopping down on the bed.

"That sound." I put my finger over my lips. Everyone stood still, listening. Then it happened again, circling around the room like a beacon.

"That's a cow. Poor cow, it's bellyaching. I hate that noise," Barbara said, putting her hands over her ears.

"What's bellyaching?"

"It's when they take the baby cow away from its mum," Barbara said.

"When they're weaned," Emma said.

The sound of two beeps came from down the street. Barbara, Polly, and Courtney stood frozen, as though the curtain were about to go up. The sound of two more beeps, short and loud, two pushes on the horn.

"It's them!" they said together, jumping up, their hands and hair flapping around like something fraying.

One by one, they climbed out of the window, grabbing the branches of the tree, a low, sturdy, safe tree right outside Barbara's window. An old apple tree for her to climb out on, late at night, to older boys waiting in a car at the end of the road.

"I'm not wearing any knickers," Courtney said as she climbed out.

Pauline, Emma, and I sat on the bed looking after them, watching them run down the road and into the back seat of the car.

The car drove off, slowly at first, then fast. We watched its lights get smaller and smaller. When they had gone, Emma pushed herself off the bed, walked over to where Barbara had dropped her pink dress, and picked it up. She held it by the shoulders and brought it up to her face as though she were smelling it.

"When do you think they'll come back?" I asked Pauline, who was still sitting on the bed, staring out of the window.

"Not till late." She picked up her overnight bag and went into the bathroom. Emma followed her, and they closed the door behind them.

I pressed my face against the cold glass of the window. I could hear the cow standing in the field, crying. It's just a cow, I told myself, it's just a cow . . . but she loves her child too. She'll forget soon, I told myself, she'll forget soon. . . .

I heard someone laugh behind me and turned around.

"You have a hole in your bottom," Pauline said, pointing.

"I know." Then I saw what it was about her that made me think of barbed wire; her small pointy teeth.

Emma and Pauline wandered around Barbara's room, looking at her things, picking them up, putting them down, trying on her clothes. They found the photograph of Jet and huddled over it, staring.

"How do you know Jet Jones?" Pauline asked, walking towards me, pulling a hairbrush through her hair. Emma stood next to her, their shoulders almost touching, turning the silver chain bracelet around her wrist.

"I don't know Jet Jones," I said. And for a moment I felt as though I couldn't move.

"What?" Pauline said, the hairbrush stuck in her hair.

They walked closer to me, both of them.

"I don't know him," I said again.

"You were making it up?" Emma asked.

I nodded. Pauline and Emma stared at me with tight smiles on their faces. I stared back at them until I felt my eyes flicker and I had to look away.

I saw Pauline give Emma a sideways look and they went into the bathroom. As they closed the bathroom door one of them said, "What a fibber!"

I turned, looking out of the window, at the branches of the trees, at the dark night, and I wished, the way you wish when you're a child, that I could fly home.

I lay down under a blanket on the floor. The light was on and I thought, I'll never fall asleep here. I counted the hours until morning; then I lay on my side and traced patterns in the rose-coloured carpet. It made my eyes feel heavy, but then the moaning came through the walls, through the windows. I stayed very still. I imagined the calf lying exhausted in a pile of hay. Lives are ruined every day, I thought. I pulled the pillow out from under my head and put it over my face and ears. That was how I fell asleep, with everything dark and muffled.

Nineteen

The sky was heavy and white when I woke. I thought, Maybe it will snow today, maybe it will snow. The other girls lay asleep around me, curled under blankets, as still as fallen stones. I lay on my back, looking up through the window at the bare branches of the trees, at the feathery hands of the evergreens. This is what it feels like to wake up next to strangers: as though you are waking up in a very cold room.

I remembered the crying sound from last night and listened for it, but it had stopped. Small birds, winter birds, landed on the thin branches of the trees, then sprang away. Everything seemed so clear against the white sky that it almost stung my eyes, but I stared and stared as though it were the first time I had ever seen anything clearly.

I sat up slowly. I had fallen asleep in my tights, and now my thighs and the back of my neck were damp from the heat. I pushed the blankets away from me and stood up. The skirt that I'd lent to Barbara lay in a pile of clothes by the side of her bed. Taking small steps on my toes I walked over to it. Being quiet is difficult, it's like holding your breath. I picked up the skirt—it smelled of cigarette smoke and perfume—and stepped into it, put on my patent leather shoes, picked up my bag. Barbara was asleep on her bed, her face half in the pillow, her straight blond hair falling around her. There were two black marks, small thumbprints, under her eyes from where her mascara had rubbed off.

I put my hand on the doorknob and held it very tightly. My head felt as though it were full of water, and I thought that I might fall down. I remembered that Mrs Whitmore had hung my coat in the peach-coloured room by the front door. I wanted to say goodbye to her, to thank her. When I looked at the Snoopy clock on Barbara's desk it was half past six. My mother was supposed to come at eleven. That's when all the mothers were supposed to collect their daughters.

The door handle made a small clanking sound, and I heard someone turn under the blankets. I froze, holding my breath, until she was still again. The only sound in the room was their breathing, slow from sleep but steady as a distant wind.

The air outside was cold. I could almost see my breath hanging thin as a moth's wing in front of me. I stopped by the side of the road to pull up my tights. It was quiet; the windows of the houses were dark. In the morning light, I saw the ditch by the side of the road. "Mind the ditch! Mind the ditch!" rang through my head like a bell. I put my hands in my pockets and walked down the narrow road, past the old brick houses and the cottages that looked like loaves of bread.

I passed a low white fence and walked close to the gate, looking for the cow I had heard last night. I stood on the fence watching; the cows grazed quietly together. The wind blew around my neck and face, lifting my hair from my shoulders. The ground was damp beneath me, and when I stepped down the mud sloshed against the sides of my shoes. I walked down the lane until I reached a crossroads and a small wooden sign posted on a telephone pole, PUBLIC FOOTPATH TO VILLAGE. An arrow pointed left.

There was a faint trail through the field from where people had walked, flattened down and darker. I had never been this way, but I wasn't worried. I followed it as though it were the only lighted path on a dark night. You can let the world take care of you if you give yourself to it. The pale wheat field spread out on either side of me, and the air smelled of leaves and fresh water. Along the sides of the field, brambles grew crooked and cracked, in bunches. I could see the tall pines and old oaks in front of me and thought, Soon my path will end at the woods. But there was another sign, just before the woods began, and a wooden gate that closed with a rope around a post. The sign said TO VILLAGE CENTRE. It pointed through the trees.

I walked into the woods and saw the narrow path winding ahead of me. It was made of earth, fallen leaves, and dried pine needles. The leaves, some almond-shaped, some the shape of rain-drops, and others as large as a handprint, felt soft underneath me. The path was overgrown in places with dark red thornbushes that caught the cloth on my coat and pulled at my tights. There were a few fallen trees right across the path and with both feet together I jumped over them. The trees became thinner, and I walked out into another, smaller field and saw the clock tower in the village.

In front of the tea house I opened my beaded change purse. It looked as though there were clouds behind the windows. I counted seventy-two pence. A bell chimed above me as I pushed the door open. It was warm inside and smelled of oatmeal. There were a few people sitting over steaming plates of eggs and mugs of tea. I sat down at a square table against the wall.

Anna, the woman whose shop it was, walked over to me. Her skirt swung below her knees, a gypsy skirt, with little silver bells on the belt.

"What would you like, little one?" She was Scottish. Her wavy reddish hair was pinned in a loose bun on the top of her head. My mother liked her; they were the same age. She had a little boy who was three years old, but she wasn't married.

"Can I have a cup of tea and a scone with strawberry jam, please?"

I cut my scone in half and buttered both sides, then spread the jam thickly on top. I poured milk in my tea and lifted the warm cup to my lips. Suddenly, I had the feeling that someone, someone who didn't like me, was watching me, and it made my stomach tight. I moved my eyes around the room, but no one was looking at me. I crossed my legs under the table and thought, The girls are probably just waking up. Emma and Pauline are telling them that I don't really know Jet, and they are sitting wide-eyed with their hands over their mouths, laughing.

"Is everything all right then?" Anna asked. There was something in her eyes that made it hard to look in them.

I nodded quickly. Then she put her hand on the top of my head. It felt warm, and the feeling in my stomach melted.

"Do you think it will snow?" I asked her. She looked like she would know. She looked as though she could tell by looking at the leaves.

"A wee bit," she said, smiling at me. "I think it will snow a bit." She stroked her hand over my head and went to clear the table across the room.

I walked home along the side of the road close to the tall beech hedges. I passed the dark brick wall that surrounded the school. The windows were dark; there was no one inside. I passed a sign that read CHRISTMAS TREES FOR SALE and said in a singsong voice, "It's almost Christmastime."

From far away I could see the whole sky and the tops of the trees reflected in the puddles, but as I walked closer they turned into muddy brown water.

My legs looked thin, and my knees seemed strange and knobby to me, but I liked the way my black patent leather shoes looked against my navy tights. I kept looking down at them as I walked.

I stared up at the trees, at the cool wide sky stretching out and out. I was alone on the road, but I wasn't afraid. I stood up straight and walked quickly ahead, as though I were being pulled closer and closer to the place where someone had said God might be.

Twenty

When I got home my mother was standing in the kitchen, wiping down the inside of the cupboard. Eden sat on the floor by the stove, holding a saucer full of milk up to the cat's mouth.

"May!" She started when she saw me. Eden looked up at me from the floor, his eyes opening wide.

"What are you doing back so early?" Her hand was on her chest; she had dropped the wet cloth on the floor. "Is everything all right?"

I thought, I'm still in the same clothes that I left in. Suddenly I had the feeling that I had forgotten something, that I had left something behind at Barbara's house or lost something in the pale yellow field.

"I woke up and couldn't get back to sleep," I said. My fingers stung from the cold, and I tried to close my hands together into a fist to warm them.

"How did you get here?"

"I walked."

There was something in her face; her eyes were moving towards me, looking closer. "It's a long way. I would have—"

"I wanted to," I told her.

There were cereal boxes, jars of jam, Marmite, and packets of tea on the counter.

"May, was the party fun?" Eden called up to me. He sat on his knees with his feet tucked under him. He was wearing striped overalls. Our grandmother had sent us matching ones.

"It was all right," I told him.

He waited a moment, then shrugged. "Oh," he said, in a low voice, and moved his hand down the cat's back, holding his fingers lightly over its coat. "May?" he asked.

"What?"

"What do you want for Christmas?"

I sat down—I still had my coat on—and placed the palms of my hands on the table. The wood felt warm and soft against my hands and I thought, Anything would feel warm against my hands right now, anything.

Outside, the sky was white and heavy. It looked as though it might suddenly fall.

"I should tell him that it's going to snow soon. He wanted to leave before it snowed, in case he got stuck."

"Tell who?" my mother asked. She had begun to put everything back in the cupboards, lining the cereal boxes up neatly next to each other like books.

"My father." Lines curved through the pale wood table like mountaintops.

"May." I heard my mother walk towards me. "I can ask him to stay if you want. He'll stay if you want, darling." Her voice was soft, but I couldn't answer. I held my breath and it stung in the middle of my throat.

I thought, You should never have to ask, you should never have to ask.

"No." I shook my head, and my hair fell over the side of my face. My wool coat felt like a shell on my back. There was a feeling in my stomach as though I had swallowed three small stones.

I heard my mother pull her chair close to mine. The table blurred in front of me, and she wrapped her arms around my shoulders. That's what made me fall. My head fell onto her chest and my shoulders rose and fell, rose and fell. My breath sounded loud to me like gasps and there was a pain in my chest, a choking feeling. I wanted him to leave, and knowing this is what pulled inside of me. It was like letting the brightest purple kite fall down from the sky.

...

My father wore a velvet suit back to London. Annabel was going back too. She had two cardboard boxes filled with the "objets" she had found at the jumble sales and markets. We walked outside to the car, which was already on and running, warming up. The air smelled of car fumes.

"I'm going to send the children's presents express post from London; it's the first thing I'm going to do after I get my vitamin shot from Tim Greenburg," Annabel said. There was a rush about her today; she flipped her hair from her shoulders. She wore a red cashmere body suit that zipped up the front and tall leather boots.

My mother pulled her cardigan tightly around herself. It was cold and the wind blew, suddenly sweeping in, then was gone again. Eden held on to the battery radio. He was listening to the news. He wanted to know if it would snow. It had only snowed once before in his life, when he was four years old.

"Did I like it?" he asked us. He wanted to hear stories about him and the snow.

"Yes," my mother said, but she wasn't looking at him. She stared at her feet, at her socks, which hung loosely off the ends of her toes. She wasn't wearing shoes.

My father looked up anxiously at the sky. I saw his brown case in the back of the car, ready to go.

" 'Bye, babes," he said, bending down to kiss me. It was early afternoon, and the sky was still bright above us. I moved one cheek towards him and then the other. When he kissed my mother goodbye on the cheek he said, pointing his finger at her, "You're missing out." He was talking about the wine bar.

"Lucy, you must come to Suzy's New Year's Eve party. You'll end up rotting away here," Annabel yelled to my mother, as she stepped in the car.

Driving away they looked like a couple, dressed up, going to the city. The city where people walked quickly down the street in raincoats, carrying umbrellas and new shopping bags, past a row of Christmas trees for sale, past clothes shops and cake shops, where streetlights shone on the damp streets. Something was happening in London tonight: a Christmas party, coins of gold light and red sweaters.

...

As we walked up the steps to the front door, my mother said, "We should buy a Christmas tree." She swung her hands out in front of her and breathed in deeply.

"Now?" Eden asked. His head bounced up like he couldn't believe it. "Today? Right now?"

"Yes," she said. A cold wind blew across us, and my mother shivered.

"As tall as May?" Eden jumped ahead up the steps to the front door.

Inside the house it seemed dark, as though it were suddenly the end of the day.

"Should we get our coats, Mum?" Eden asked.

She walked towards the stairs but stopped suddenly and stood looking at the grey-blue stone floor.

"Mum?"

"What, darling?" she touched the back of her neck with her hand.

"When are we getting the Christmas tree?"

"In a minute." When I was younger I really believed that a minute meant one minute, but now I knew it could be hours. It could even be days.

"Mum?" Eden said again, looking at her. She stood very still, as if she were trying to hear something.

Eden let out a loud breath and dropped his shoulders.

I looked up at the ceilings, which were high and curved, and wrapped my arms around myself. It was as cold as a church. I started to walk towards the stairs, but my footsteps sounded like a laugh underneath me and I stopped. We were quiet and standing still, each of us turning slowly inside our own rings, as lost and alone as the planets.

...

As I walked upstairs I saw my mother, through the bars in the banister, walk down the hall towards the back of the house.

Eden and I went to the kitchen. We cut thick pieces of bread and made butter-and-cheese sandwiches. We stood up while we ate, and I thought of all the things the girls would say about me. When we were done, Eden said, "May, what are you going to do now?"

"Nothing." I started walking out the door.

"Oh." He held the crust of his sandwich in his hand.

"You can come in my room if you want," I told him.

We put the radio on the floor and found the programme we liked. It was playing the usual songs and some rock 'n' roll Christmas carols.

"Are you tired?" Eden asked me. I was lying on my side thinking about Barbara's house, about Emma and Pauline standing side by side. What I was really thinking about was myself, and why I wasn't afraid.

I thought about when we were dancing and the way that Mr Whitmore looked. It made me laugh out loud.

"Why did you just laugh?" Eden asked.

I did a forward somersault on my bed. Eden watched; he liked to watch me. I did another one. I could feel my face flush.

"Do you want me to teach you the new dance I learned?"

He nodded.

"Stand up and turn the radio up!" I said, jumping up.

I did the Bus Stop while he watched, but then another song we liked came on the radio and we both danced in our own way. I stepped from side to side, snapping my fingers, and Eden jumped in the air and spun around. Our faces were turning red and we had to take off our sweaters. Outside it grew darker and darker. Then we had a spinning contest. I won. Standing in the middle of the room with our arms stretched out at our sides, looking up at the ceiling, turning and turning and turning, then collapsing on the floor while the room spun around us. And the whole time I was thinking, What's wrong with me? Why aren't I afraid?

We couldn't find our mother. Eden and I went from room to room looking for her. Then we decided to look downstairs.

"But we have to go in the dark," I told Eden, and he made a shivering sound. We put our socks and sweaters back on because we knew it would be colder downstairs and started down the narrow pitch-black staircase. Eden held on to the back of my shirt. I wasn't scared, even though it was dark, because I knew it was only seven o'clock. The house moved around us as we walked through it, back and forth, like an old ship.

"Mum! Mummy!" Our voices sounded strange and hollow against the stone walls downstairs. When there was no answer, we became very quiet as we walked from room to room. Then we found her, curled on her side, asleep on the bed in the room that Rufus had stayed in. We watched her from the door. I remembered once when I woke her up she said, "I wish you hadn't woken me. I was having the nicest dream."

"Don't wake her up," I said to Eden, as he started towards her. "Let's have a race upstairs!" We raced to the hallway and up the stairs. I won.

In the kitchen, I poured milk into a speckled blue-and-white pot and put it on the stove. We pulled the tin down from the top shelf and took two Penguin bars out, one each. I mixed chocolate syrup into the warm milk. We went to the sitting room, walking very slowly, with our hands wrapped around the mugs and the Penguin bars in our pockets. We turned on the lights and stood by the side of the telly turning the knob—it was stiff and ticked like a clock—from programme to programme. ITV was Parliament, BBC 2 was a programme we called *How to Build a Bridge*, but BBC 1 was *Top of the Pops*.

"It's *Top of the Pops!*" I said, jumping up and down.

"It's *Top of the Pops!*" Eden said, jumping up and down. It was warm in the sitting room and full of music, glitter, and lights from the telly. When we knew the words to the songs, we jumped up and sang along with the girls and boys who were dancing and waving their hands in the air on the show.

That's what we did for the rest of the night, sat on the sofa watching telly and during the adverts we ran down the hallway, leaping and skipping to the kitchen, where we pulled a chair to the cupboards and stood on it reaching far back for the hidden sweet tin.

Once, when we were sitting on the sofa unwrapping the foil from our third Penguin bars, we heard what sounded like a footstep, a creak in the doorway. We both jumped, thinking it was our mother, covering the chocolate with our hands. But when we looked, peeking out of the doorway, there was no one there. It was just the house making noises.

Twenty-one

"May, it's snowing!" I felt Eden's hand on my shoulder, gently pushing me awake. "May, it snowed last night. It snowed!"

A dull, flat light came through the closed curtains. I thought I was waking up in London. I lay on my side with my eyes open looking at the windows, at the blue flowers on the cream-coloured curtains that hung to the floor. I thought, I'll see rooftops and chimneys when I open them. I'll see the city. Then I remembered I was in my mother's room.

Last night Eden and I fell asleep on the sofa in the sitting room. In the middle of the night I heard footsteps coming up the stairs, each step a slow thud. I lay on my back in the dark, my eyes wide open, arms stiff at my sides. I have always been afraid of something, of someone. I always knew something would happen to me, to all of us, and now it was about to. A man with a beard, holding a knife or a metal stick, was coming to kill us. Eden was asleep at the other end of the sofa. I kicked his feet to wake him, but he rolled over. The light in the hall went on and the floorboards creaked just outside the door. I thought, He's about to kill us. I saw the shadow cross the wall—and then my mother walked in and gently covered us with a blanket.

I couldn't get back to sleep. The kitchen light was on. My mother was sitting at the table writing something on a plain white piece of paper.

"Mum."

Her hair hung over her face. There was a brown knitted hat next to her. When she finally looked up, her eyes were red and watery. "Did I wake you?"

"I have a stomach ache," I said, looking at the dark window.

"That's because you ate all the chocolate. I'll make you some camomile tea." She went to the kettle. "Did anyone phone while I was asleep?" she asked.

"No." I walked closer to the table, to the place where she had left the paper. It read:

Dear Rufus,
I found your brown hat in your room. You must have
forgotten it, so I'm sending it back to you. I also wanted to

The rest was scribbled over.

She sat with me on her bed while I took tiny sips of the hot tea. When she left I closed my eyes and thought, Soon I'll fall asleep, soon I'll be sleeping. But there were sounds from the kitchen, the clink of china and the boiling kettle. I heard my mother walking around, the bathwater running. Finally, I must have fallen asleep in my mother's bed.

Eden opened the curtains to show me the snow. It was coming down lightly, thinly, against the grey sky. The tops of the trees were white and perfectly still. I stared at it, at the snow slowly falling, floating down quiet as feathers. I remembered the way Rufus laid his hand on my mother's shoulder, on the small of her back, and I thought, I have never seen anything move so softly, anything fall so softly.

My mother made boiled eggs and toast for breakfast. We sat at the table and watched the snow. She wiped the table with a yellow sponge. She was wearing the same clothes as yesterday. Everything moved so slowly.

"Maybe I should phone Rufus about the hat?" She opened her address book that had come undone at the spine and turned through the loose pages.

"Mum, when are we going to get the Christmas tree?" Eden asked, but she didn't answer. She was already dialling, pulling each number around. She held the black, serious-looking phone against her ear. I could hear it ring. Ringing and ringing in an empty room. I saw her look up at the clock; it was almost ten. When she put the phone down her eyes went over to the window and I thought, She is imagining Rufus waking up in a cosy flat in London with shells around the edges of a perfectly clean bathtub. Patricia's flat.

...

In London, in the middle of the night, in the middle of December, big lorries come from the country piled high with Christmas trees. One man stands on top and throws the trees down to the man standing on the ground. They land with a thump, and ice sparkles fly from them like light.

Here, we followed the signs posted to the trees and lampposts that read CHRISTMAS TREES FOR SALE. An arrow pointed down a dirt lane. My mother pulled over on the side of the road and turned the key. "Maybe we should go to London for Christmas."

Outside we could see the Christmas trees planted in rows, dark green and lightly covered with snow, waving in the soft wind.

"Who would we stay with?"

She shrugged. "Suzy, Annabel. . . . It would probably be more fun than just sitting around here. There'll be parties and other people." Christmas at one of her friends' flats in London: men in faded jeans and long hair, a piece of incense burning in a red clay dish.

"I don't care," I said. It was getting cold in the car. I put my hands under my legs.

The ground was covered with the thinnest layer of snow, so thin you could see the shape of everything underneath, even the leaves and the smallest stones.

"Please, Mum. Can we just get a Christmas tree?" Eden said from the back seat. His voice was soft, and he looked as though he might cry.

...

Our tree was small and there was a gap in the side, but at the top baby pinecones grew from the branches, as though the tree were decorating itself.

"None of the other trees had them, did they?" Eden asked, looking up at us. Everyone wants to have something special, the only one like it, and Eden wanted a Christmas that is really like a Christmas.

We took the dusty boxes filled with ornaments out of the hall cupboard. Eden unwrapped the Tin Man from its tissue paper— it was his favourite, even though it was missing an arm—and hung it on the tree. I stood on my toes to hang the silver, glittery half-moon.

"Mum?" Eden wanted her to hang the tiny white snowman at the top of the tree. She didn't hear him. She was sitting by herself on the sofa, with one leg crossed over the other, writing words with her finger on the wooden table.

The phone rang and she jumped, staring at it, letting it ring one more time. When she picked it up she said "Hello," very slowly.

"Oh, hello, Mummy," she said. "Yes we did, thank you very much. I've hidden them." It was my grandmother, phoning from America.

"Hi, Granny." My voice echoed on the line; it made me stop talking before I had finished the end of each sentence.

"The streets are covered with snow; it's a real blizzard," my grandmother told me, her voice clean and crisp. I imagined her tree decorated only with tiny white lights and red bows, standing on an oriental rug in her New York apartment, her American husband sitting in a chair, a glass filled halfway with Scotch and ice cubes in his hand, a plate of cheese and crackers on the dark wood table at his side.

When Eden got on the phone he said, "We have a Christmas tree now!"

I saw my mother standing by the tree, but she wasn't hanging any ornaments or even looking at them. Her eyes were drifting somewhere else in between the branches of the tree. I wondered if she had bought us any presents yet. I pulled the phone away from Eden.

"Can I come to America for Christmas, Granny? I don't want to be here with Mum." In her apartment there would be shopping bags on the floor, store-wrapped presents under the tree, her purse with the curved bamboo handle on the kitchen table, a suit jacket with gold buttons hanging off the back of a chair.

"Next year, May. I hope the present fits you," she said, and blew a kiss over the phone. It was clothes. Nothing is ever a surprise.

"Do you think I should put the rocking horse here or here?" Eden asked our mother, holding it in the two different places to show her. But she was staring at me.

"That wasn't a very nice thing to say. Why don't you want to spend Christmas with me?" Her voice shook and her eyes looked glassy.

"Well, you haven't been trying to make this a very good Christmas," I said, turning away from her. "Here, Eden." I pointed to the spot where I thought the rocking horse ornament looked better.

She walked over to us, to where we were, moving around the tree, the tree that was everything to us then, the tree that shone and sparkled and stretched out its arms for more.

"I was going to take you shopping tomorrow." When she said that, Eden got excited and jumped up and down; tomorrow was a gift to him.

I picked up the robin's-nest ornament and hung it carefully on a branch near the top of the tree. My mother knelt down, look- .
ing through the boxes, and pulled out a glittering icicle. Tissue paper and boxes were scattered around us, I sat down on the floor next to the tree and cleaned the silver bells with my shirt. We were making it perfect, this tree.

Twenty-two

The next morning we drove into Shepperton to do our Christmas shopping. A layer of snow covered the fields and roofs but the roads were clear; they stretched out dark and wet ahead of us. Our mother had woken us up early.

"Come on, you two, let's get a move on," she had said, standing over us in her beige coat, while Eden and I tied our shoes. It made me confused, and I had to tie them again. "I want to get there before the crowds," she said, but really she just wanted to leave the house.

The High Street was a hill of shops. My mother parked at the bottom, near the bank.

"I just have to pop into the bank first," she said, as we got out of the car. The clouds were moving quickly above us, leaving plain blue sky behind them.

"I'm going shopping by myself," I told her. I opened my hands to feel the wind blow through them, but there was none.

"May, can I come with you?" Eden asked, looking up at me. "I have ten pounds." I had money too; our grandmother sent it to us for our birthdays and for Christmas with instructions to buy our mother something nice.

"Where should I meet you?" our mother asked us. I looked up at her, but I could hardly see her. The sun was in my eyes and her face was getting lost in the blue sky, in the rushing clouds.

"We'll take the bus home," I said.

"All right."

I saw my mother start to run across the street, but she stopped in the middle of the road and looked back at us. I heard the horn of a car and then the short squealing sound of brakes. I thought, Now I'll see her fall, straight down, the way a tree falls, the way a ladder falls. When the car stopped my mother was still standing, right in front of it, her coat touching the bumper. She waved and mouthed, "Sorry," to the driver, then came running towards us.

"Are you sure you don't want me to pick you up later? I'll meet you somewhere."

But Eden and I had already started up the hill, towards the shops.

We looked in every window of every shop, even the hairdresser and the newsagent, just to see. Shepperton was the biggest town, and everyone from the villages did their shopping here. When we asked our mother what she wanted for Christmas, she had said, "Socks."

We passed a shop full of glass bottles with silver tops and soaps wrapped in cellophane and ribbons. It smelled of lavender inside. The women in the store looked like my grandmother, hair brushed down smooth, a hair band or combs holding it neatly back. I spent a long time smelling the soaps and creams. Eden picked out a tall cloudy green-glass bottle. Everything had little silver and purple tags describing what was inside; this was lily-scented hand cream.

When we came out of the shop, carrying our bottle of lily hand cream in a white paper bag with bluebells printed on it, the sun was coming out and the streets were becoming full. A woman who looked like Barbara's mother walked out of the men's outfitters carrying two shop-wrapped parcels. I held Eden by the wrist as we passed a group of teenage boys and girls standing outside the record shop, smoking cigarettes. One of the girls, with dyed red hair, held her hand on her stomach, laughing.

We stopped at the café and bought watercress sandwiches and two bottles of orangeade and sat at a little round table. The sun came in bright through the windows. I heard the voice of an old man behind us say, "It's a warm day for December." It was a warm day for December. All the snow must have melted by now.

We looked in the bakery window. It smelled of sweet buns. "Which is your favourite?" Eden asked me. I pointed to a yellow fairy cake with a pink flower on top. I thought I saw Jolene inside the crowded shop. I pushed my face closer to the warm glass, but when the girl turned her face towards us it was somebody else, a girl I'd never seen before. I remembered walking slowly down the corridor at school, running my finger along the lines in the bricks. When I looked back at the cakes I wasn't hungry any more.

"We'll get something later," I said, and started walking to the top of the hill where the stone church sat, old and alone, in a garden. There was a tall Christmas tree by the church decorated in coloured lights. People sat on benches with the tops of their prams down. Eden and I walked around the tree; it would never fit in a house. The ground was damp from where the snow had melted. Two boys, a few years older than Eden, ran around the tree hitting it with sticks. They both wore matching brown jumpers and had thick brown hair and freckles. There was something about the older boy's mouth; it looked as though he were biting something hard.

We walked back down the street. It was getting cooler now, the clouds coming in. People were looking up at the sky, to see if it would rain.

We went to the sweetshop at the bottom of the road by the bus stop. We each took a small white paper bag and walked between the glass jars. A pretty young mother with black hair and hazel eyes leaned her arm on the counter, watching her three sons as they knelt down to look in the jars of sweets. "Harry, Jack, and Sam. I love my three boys," she said to the man behind the counter.

I knew what I wanted: jelly babies, lemon sherbets, and a rhubarb and cream lolly. We bought Mum a small bag of black-currant-and-licorice sweets and some pear drops; she liked them even though they tasted of nail varnish. We would put them in her Christmas stocking with the socks. There were glass jars of different-coloured sweets everywhere; some were just plain orange, mint and pineapple.

I walked back and forth on the edge of the pavement while we waited for the bus, a lemon drop in my mouth. If I didn't fall, it was good luck, like a found penny, something to believe in. I looked around for Eden. He was standing under a tree, his head back, looking up at the branches.

As the bus drove away from town the streets became narrower, winding through the villages like a black snake.

Two women sat behind us, talking about their children and who made a better Christmas pudding.

"Why were you staring at that tree?"

Eden looked at me. He was chewing on a toffee, his lips wet and pink. He shrugged, swinging his legs under the seat.

"Can I have one of your chocolate mice?" I asked him. I held the bag with the glass bottle of hand cream on my lap.

He shook his head, not looking at me, poking through his bag of sweets. "I only have two left," he said.

"Give me one," I said, leaning forward, whispering in his ear because the bus was full and my voice sounded like something about to burn. "I took you shopping, Eden." I held my hand out.

Eden looked away, out of the window, but I didn't move. Finally he gave me one, slapping it down in my palm.

Behind us I heard one of the women ask the other, "Is your daughter coming over for Christmas?"

"No," the other woman said. "I don't think she will."

"Oh. That's a pity."

"Yes."

I looked out of the window. We passed a low stone wall. This is what it is like between villages: fields and a farm, a house with one light on.

"Well, she'll put something nice in the post for you, then." This woman had a voice that could turn corners, creep under the door to find something out, then put it in her purse.

"My daughter's never given me a present in her life," the other woman said to her.

I turned my head slowly, to look behind me, as though I were scratching my cheek on my shoulder.

She had a small face and grey hair, tied in a bun. Her back rounded over and her shoulders came forward, piercing through her cream-coloured cardigan like two sharp rocks. But it wasn't because she was old that her back rounded over. Deep in the hollow of her chest, she was safely keeping the rest of her heart, the last red stone of it. Oh, I thought, and the words went through my mind slowly, that's what happens to the heart, that's what can happen.

Then it was our stop. The bus doors opened and the air blew in, damp and smelling of the sea.

Eden and I walked home along the side of the road. A few cars passed, slowing down when they saw us. I remembered a glass box that I had seen somewhere. It was big enough to keep little things: rings and hair clips. In between the glass were pressed, dried flowers with long thin blue and purple petals.

"Tomorrow I want to find something else for Mum," I said to Eden. He was walking towards a row of branches that were growing straight up from the ground, like rods; on the top were dark red bulbs. They looked like something from another time. Eden stood looking up at them, the way he had done at the bus stop.

"What are you doing?"

"I'm trying to see the leaves breathing."

...

We hid our mother's presents in the back of my wardrobe.

When we walked into the kitchen, it looked as though we were going to have a party. There was a wooden box filled with clementines on the table, IMPORTED FROM SPAIN stamped on the side; a wedge of Brie surrounded by water crackers, on a blue-and-white flowered plate; and a Christmas cake in a tin. Like a party, I thought, just like a party.

"Did you two have fun without your mum?" she asked, in a silly voice.

Eden ran to her and wrapped his arms around her legs. "Did you find the Lego rocket set?"

"The Lego what? What's that? I don't think I've ever heard of that," she said, teasing him.

"Mum!"

She bent down to cuddle him; he put his hands on her cheeks.

"You've got sticky hands, Eden. You've been eating sweets again." She moved his hands from her face.

"We had a sandwich first," I said.

There was a string of Christmas cards that my mother had hung up along the window.

"Guess what I bought?" my mother asked, opening her eyes wide.

"Are those all the Christmas cards we've had?" I looked at them, hanging like laundry over the sink. There were only five.

My mother looked back at them, over her shoulder. "We'll get more," she said.

Things like that are important, how many people send you Christmas cards.

"What did you buy, Mum?" Eden asked.

"A Christmas cake. I thought we could make icing for it and decorate it; you like doing things like that, May."

I nodded. "Did you remember the marzipan?"

"Yes, and the little silver balls." She pulled out a plastic bag from the cupboard. In it were the cake decorations.

"Clear a spot and we'll make the icing," she said.

She took the measuring cup down from the cupboard, the eggs from the fridge, and the icing sugar and put them on the table.

She read the recipe out loud, and I poured the icing sugar into the measuring cup.

"What can I do?" Eden asked. He was sitting at the table, resting his chin on his hands.

"Get a wooden spoon."

The phone rang. My mother jumped up, quickly, as though something had just pinched her on the bottom.

Eden and I watched her as she picked up the phone, taking a breath in, waiting a moment, like a wish, before she said, "Hello."

"Hello, darling. . . . I'm just phoning to see if the parcel arrived." It was Annabel. I could hear her voice coming through receiver.

"It hasn't come today."

"The post is up the wall these days. . . ."

I took the blue-and-white mixing bowl from the cupboard and put it on the table. Eden was standing outside the door, with the wooden spoon in his hand, looking down the hallway. I tried to take the whisk out of the drawer, but it got stuck and wouldn't open when I pulled the handle. The whisk, the spoons, and the spatulas all rattled together.

"I think someone's ringing the bell," Eden said. I followed him down the hallway. My mother was still on the phone. Eden and I stood very quietly listening; the bell had been fixed, but it was still hard to hear. Then it came, the light buzzing sound of the front doorbell.

"It's the postman!" I said, and we hurried down the stairs. I worried that he might have been ringing for a long time and would leave before we got there.

The first thing I saw when I opened the door were the black buttons on his coat.

"Hello, May," he said. I looked past him at the bare hedge against the white and blue sky. A damp wind blew against my face and neck, and I opened the door all the way.

"Hello, Rufus," I said. He stepped into the dark hall, slowly, carefully.

"Rufus, do you have a Christmas tree?" Eden asked, when he saw him. He had just come down the stairs.

"No, I don't," Rufus said, laughing.

"Oh, because we have one now," Eden said, as he skipped towards him.

"My mother's upstairs," I said.

"I wanted to talk to her."

"She's on the phone," I told him. He was looking up at the staircase, where my mother was standing, holding on to the banister.

"Lucy, I hope you don't mind that I came by like this, but I wanted to talk to you. . . ."

"No, I don't mind," she said, shaking her head. "Where did you come from?"

"London. I drove this time."

"Well, would you like to have a cup of tea . . . ?" Each word she said sounded unsure, as though she were speaking in another language.

"Yes, thank you. I would."

Eden and I followed them upstairs into the kitchen. My mother lifted the kettle from the stove and filled it from the tap. Rufus unbuttoned his coat and put it over the back of a chair.

"Would you like something to eat?" my mother asked.

"I'm not very hungry."

No one spoke. The only sound was the fire from the stove. Then Rufus asked, "Are Annabel and Simon still here?"

"No. They went back to London."

Eden and I sat down at the table. We opened the bag of cake decorations. There was a miniature Father Christmas, a sleigh with reindeer, and a snowman. We put them on our cake every year and decorated the rest with silver balls and holly and sometimes other sweets that we would stick on the icing.

My mother handed Rufus a cup of tea. They both sipped their tea standing up. Outside, the sky was turning a darker blue. You could hear, when we were all still and quiet, the sound of the waves hitting the rocks below.

"You left your hat here," my mother said to him.

"My hat?"

I opened the marzipan wrapper; we would have to roll it flat and wrap it around the cake, underneath the icing. Eden stuck his finger in the icing sugar.

"That's not the reason I came back. Lucy, I wanted to talk to you."

Some people need to be told like that, and even then they still don't believe. They hold on to their heart so tightly that it can't hear.

"I wanted to give you this," Rufus said, and he held out his arm to her. I thought, What is it? In his hand he held a folded piece of paper. She put her tea down and took a step, slowly reaching out her hand towards his.

Eden was making a marzipan cat, pinching up the ears, rolling out the tail.

"Eden, we need that for the cake," I said, but then I started to make one too.

I heard the crinkling sound of the paper in my mother's hands as she unfolded it. Rufus looked away.

She seemed to hold it for a long time, looking down at it, not speaking. Rufus put his hand around the back of the chair. His eyes went from the floor to her: to her hands, to her face. Eden and I worked on our marzipan animals, pretending to concentrate, but really we were both quietly watching.

When she had read the letter, she refolded it and walked over to the sink. She stood at the window, underneath the hanging Christmas cards, holding it tightly between both hands. Her lips began to tremble and she brought her fingers to her mouth, as if to still them. The room was quiet. No one spoke. No one moved. The only sound was my mother's crying.

...

Later, I found the note in my mother's jewellery box.

> *Dear Lucy,*
> *This is the translation of the note: "The key to my locked spirit is your laughing mouth." That is what I have always felt, what the truth has always been.*
>
> *Love,*
> *Rufus*

We walked over the rocks and down to the beach below. The sky was pale blue and the air was cool. We had our long winter coats and scarves on. My mother and Rufus walked side by side, talking, their hands in their pockets. Eden ran ahead, picking up stones and shells out of the wet sand and rinsing them in the sea.

The tide was coming in; the waves rose and fell slowly, as though they were tired and wanted to sleep. Seagulls flew above us, landing on the shore. I felt the sand underneath me and thought, How could I have ever been afraid of this world, which has given me everything I need?

"Look!" Eden shouted. He was farther down the beach, pointing to a pile of seaweed that had washed ashore.

My mother looked at Rufus and they both smiled, almost starting to laugh. Then she said, trying to sound serious, "What is it, Eden?"

"There's a starfish in the seaweed!" he shouted back excitedly.

We walked over to look. The starfish was tangled in the green and stringy seaweed. Eden knelt down and carefully picked it out. He stood up, holding the small, sand-coloured animal in the palm of his hand.

We waited, looking at it. It was young with thin arms, it sat frozen in Eden's hand. I touched it with my finger. It felt cold and rubbery, like a dog's nose, but it didn't move.

"It's not moving," Eden said, his face fallen. "It's probably dead."

"Put it in the water," Rufus said. "Maybe it will come back to life."

We found a small pool of water at the bottom of the rocks. The starfish dropped lifeless to the bottom.

"Oh . . ." Eden said, his hand dropping to the sand, as he watched it fall. He put some shells in for decoration and a piece of seaweed for it to eat.

"You have to wait a minute," my mother said.

A cool wind blew in from the ocean, and my mother made a shivering sound.

"Are you cold?" Rufus asked.

"A bit."

He wrapped his arms around her, and she rested her head gently on his shoulder. That's what it looks like to be held in the arms of someone who loves you: soft as sleep and as pure as the moon.

Two seagulls circled above us, making a sound. Eden looked up at them, worried.

"They might try to eat it," he said, covering the small pool of water with his hands.

"No, they won't. Don't worry, Eden," I told him. I knew they wouldn't like it, it would be too gummy and hard to swallow.

I dipped my fingers in the clear water, then touched them to my forehead, like a blessing. I put one finger in my mouth and tasted the cold water and salt.

"I think it just moved," Eden said, putting his head closer so his nose almost touched the water.

I looked down at the pale green water, at the small shells and stones, at the floating pieces of seaweed. At first I thought it was just the water moving over it, so I stared without blinking, to see if it would happen again.

"Yes, it's moving!" I said. It seemed to be waving its arms, swimming over the rocks and shells.

"It's alive!" Eden said, looking at me, his eyes wide. He jumped up, smiling and yelling.

We saw our mother and Rufus walking hand in hand farther down the beach. The sky was still light and pale blue above us; the wind blew in softly from the ocean. Eden ran towards them, shouting.

"Mum! Rufus! The starfish is alive!" The seagulls on the shore flew up and away from him as he ran, yelling. "The starfish is alive! The starfish is alive!"

Acknowledgments

I would like to thank the following people a thousand times: Joe Dolce and Jonathan Burnham for reading this manuscript and recommending me to my agent.

Kim Witherspoon, whom I somehow knew would be the best agent for this book, and I am thankful, every day, that she is. She guided it quickly and smoothly into the perfect hands.

Elisabeth Schmitz, for her thoughtful, careful edits which refined this book. I could not have imagined working with such a caring and respected editor and am continually aware of how lucky I am.

Morgan Entrekin, Judy Hottensen, Charles Woods, Deb Seager and Molly Boren at Grove/Atlantic where I feel that I'm in such good hands I don't have to worry about a thing.

Felicity Rubinstein, for so enthusiastically representing this manuscript in England.

Dan Franklin, my editor at Jonathan Cape, whom I am honoured to be working with.

Mary Gordon who taught me to choose words carefully, to read closely and to work hard. Connie Budelis and the Barnard English department for letting me take Mary's writing class every semester.

New York University's creative writing program and *The New York Times* fellowship. My teachers: Susanna Moore for her friendship and guidance, Mona Simpson for teaching us to take our writing seriously, and E. L. Doctorow for telling me to, "Press on."

Lyn Chase for her interest in my writing since I was eighteen.

Ami Armstrong for her helpful advice.

Gideon Weil, Joshua Greenhut and Maria Massie at the Witherspoon agency for their continued kindness even before I was a client there.

My mother Sophy Craze, for reading this draft by draft, chapter by chapter, and for patiently correcting my spelling and punctuation.

My friends who read this manuscript along the way and offered encouragement: Christina Wayne, Holly Dando, Lizzy Simon, Elizabeth Yost Song, Nora Chassler, Amber Lasciak, Meg Thomson, David Grand, Rebecca Abbott, Anna VanLenten and Jett Craze.

Harry Joseph for finding the starfish.